THE STREETS NEVER LET GO

Lock Down Publications and Ca$h
Presents
THE STREETS NEVER LET GO
A Novel by *Robert Baptiste*

The Streets Never Let Go

Lock Down Publications
Po Box 944
Stockbridge, Ga 30281

Visit our website @
www.lockdownpublications.com

Copyright 2021 by Robert Baptiste
The Streets Never Let Go

*This is a work of fiction. Names, characters, places, and incidents either
are products of the author's imagination or are used fictitiously. Any
similarity to actual events or locales or persons, living or dead, is
entirely coincidental.*

Lock Down Publications
Like our page on Facebook: Lock Down Publications @
www.facebook.com/lockdownpublications.ldp

Book interior design by: **Shawn Walker**
Edited by: **Nuel Uyi**

Stay Connected with Us!

Text **LOCKDOWN** to 22828 to stay up-to-date with new releases, sneak peaks, contests and more…
Thank you.

Submission Guideline.

Submit the first three chapters of your completed manuscript to ldpsubmissions@gmail.com, subject line: Your book's title. The manuscript must be in a .doc file and sent as an attachment. Document should be in Times New Roman, double spaced and in size 12 font. Also, provide your synopsis and full contact information. If sending multiple submissions, they must each be in a separate email.

Have a story but no way to send it electronically? You can still submit to LDP/Ca$h Presents. Send in the first three chapters, written or typed, of your completed manuscript to:

LDP: Submissions Dept
Po Box 944
Stockbridge, Ga 30281

DO NOT send original manuscript. Must be a duplicate.

Provide your synopsis and a cover letter containing your full contact information.

Thanks for considering LDP and Ca$h Presents.

About The Author

Robert Baptiste is from New Orleans, Louisiana.

He served 14 years in Federal Prison where he began his writing career. A lot of his stories are from of his street life.

Robert Baptiste is home now, living in New Orleans where he continues to write the heat for the streets. You can check him out on Facebook at *Robert Baptiste* or IG at *Robert 504 Baptiste*. Follow him and let him know what you think about his books.

And make sure you check out his other books on Lockdown Publishing—especially his blockbuster titled *Caught Up in The Life*, which has won five stars on Amazon.com

Dedication

To all the fallen rappers in the city of New Orleans and around the world.

RIP to Slim and the rest of the rappers in the city.

Robert Baptiste

Prologue

"Fuck! Yea, Slim, give me this dick."

I had this fine bitch named Poo out the Calliope on all fours, slamming my dick in and out of her wet pussy. "Damn! This pussy good," I said, slapping her on the ass.

"I'm coming! Slim! I'm coming." She climbed on top of me, bouncing up and down, riding my dick, biting down on her bottom lip.

"Shit! Shit! This dick is good." She pressed down on my chest with her hands, riding me even harder as she came.

I flipped her over on her side, fucking the shit out of her.

"Yea, daddy, give me that dick."

I got in the middle of her, holding one of her legs up in the air as I slammed deeper and harder into her pussy. "I'm about to nut. I'm about to nut." I shivered as she pushed back on me.

"I'm about to come too," she said, shaking.

We came at the same time. I shot my nut in her, as she came all over my dick. I fell on the bed, trying to catch my breath. She went into the bathroom.

A few minutes later I fell asleep.

I woke up around 4 o'clock. "Damn! I'm tripping," I muttered under my breath. I looked at her. She was knocked out asleep.

I grabbed my clothes from the floor and put them on. Then I grabbed my gun and keys, and walked out. As I was coming out the dark hallway in the Calliope Projects, with my gun under my arm, headed to my truck, I saw a shadow coming from behind a dumper. In the blink of an eye, the person fired several shots at me from a pistol.

I couldn't even react.

I felt the hot bullets ripping through my clothes.

I took a couple of bullets in the legs and arms. I fell back against the truck and slid down.

Then he stood over me, shooting me in the head.

That was the last thing I remembered before it went dark.

And I heard Bond's voice: "You can't have one foot in and

one foot out."

Chapter 1

Slim

1990

Here I am, in Uptown Third Ward, standing in the dark hallway of the Willow St. Courtway in the Magnolia Projects. I'm dressed in all-black Reeboks, from my bandanna down to my sneakers, with my black 9mm Glock in my waist. I'm selling rocks and smoking on a blunt loaded off of dope.

In the Magnolia, you can't trust nobody. The Magnolia is one of most treacherous and cut-throat projects in New Orleans. Where niggas keep their heat on them at all times. Especially where I'm from: the 6 Court—The Circle.

That's the side of the Magnolia Project where the killers live.

All the lights are shot out in the courtway, dope fiends, crack heads and stray dogs running around.

It's a place where niggas keep their AK-47s (or (choppers, which is our slang word for this type of gun) laying in the grass or in the hallways.

And they stay beef with niggas from all over the city, because they probably pulled off a jack move.

It's normal in my project to see niggas hanging out strapped up, hustling, getting money or engaged in a shoot-out with motherfuckers.

It's nothing to walk out your front in the projects and see a dead body, or dope fiends who perforated themselves with needles, even crack pipe users and motherfuckers O.D.'ing on heroin.

I clenched my gun when I saw a crackhead walking toward me.

"What's up, Slim?" Anna said.

"What good?"

"You got something?"

"Yea. What you want?"

"Two dimes."

I pulled the plastic bag from under my nuts that had about a thousand dollars' worth of rocks in it. I opened it up, serving her. "Here you go."

She handed me two tens. "Thanks," she said, walking off.

This cracks shit is cool. But I like hitting licks. Robbing and jacking niggas for keys and money.

I walked upstairs to my mother's apartment. We've been living in the Magnolia as long as I can remember. I got pushed out my mother's pussy at Charity Hospital and straight to the Magnolia Projects.

I spent seventeen years as a Magnolia 6 Court representative from slinging iron to beefing over wars.

When I jumped off the porch back in the game, the O.G taught me how to be stand-up; as in, don't never rat on somebody, take my lick and never let a nigga play me or disrespect me.

I walked in my room, putting my gun on the dresser along with the crack.

I grabbed the half blunt out the ashtray lifting it up. I took a hit of the blunt, blowing smoke out my nose and mouth. I grabbed the note pad, turning the track on, bopping my head, writing a verse down. This rap thing is cool, but it ain't bring in no money.

It just real something I'm fucking around in the projects with.

One day I was in the Circle—what we call the 6 Court. This was where I jumped off the porch at. At the age of twelve I jumped in the game, selling rocks. One day in the circle, they had a DJ. People bucked me up to get on the mic and rip it. And I'd been fucking with it off and on ever since.

But like I said, it don't put no money in my pockets.

Plus the type of music I write, nigga ain't real feeling it. And niggas not on the level. Everybody can't feel real shit, because every nigga ain't real.

I've done more as a teenager than a nigga have done their whole life.

I grabbed the foil pack off the dresser, snorting it, laid back on the bed, letting the snort hit me. "Damn. This fire." I first got introduced to heroin through my brother—June. He also was one of the O.G niggas that taught me the game. From selling dope to killing motherfuckers. Now he's serving a life sentence in Angola State Penitentiary for some murders. He was a hit man for a lot of major drug dealers in the city.

***

Slim

I got up the next evening, getting in the shower. As I was about to get out of the shower, my mother knocked on the door.
"Slim, I cooked."
"Okay." I walked in my room, slid on some black boxers, black wife beater, blue Girbauds, and some black Reeboks. I draped my white polo over my shoulder.
I walked in the kitchen, kissing my mother. My mother was thick, dark-skinned, with black short hair, and a round pie face. You could tell she was fine back in the game, with four open face golds in her mouth. She used to fuck with baller niggas in the game. My father was one in the Magnolia. The police killed him in a shoot-out.
I sat at the table. "Here." She gave me a plate of red beans and fried chicken. My mother was a nurse at an old folks' home.
Just then somebody knocked at the door.
"Who is it?" I said, walking to the door.
"Tre."
"What's up, my nigga?" I dapped him off.
"Come in and get some of this food," my mother said.
"Yes, Ms. Mays." Tre was my best friend since the sand box days. We jumped off the porch together, and pulled off jacks and murders together.
Tre is light-skinned, 5'6 pretty boy type nigga with good wavy hair, but he's about his business.
"I'm gone to work," my mother said, walking out the door.
"Love."

13

"Be safe."

"Okay, mom."

We went into my room.

"Here." Light this up. I passed Tre the blunt.

"Man, listen to this track," I said, playing him the song I had recorded.

"Man, that shit sound live."

"This some shit to make them hoes shake their ass to."

"You going to rock this at *Club 49*?" Tre said, blowing the smoke out his nose.

"Yea, understand me—Nigga we need a lick," I said, snorting a bag of coke.

"Shit. This shit in the 8 ward—I'm working on it."

"Okay."

"Yea, these nigga playing with a couple bricks."

"A'ight. I need that shit. My pockets on hurt."

"Me too."

"Nigga, let's bust a move. I need to go get a bag of dope to kill this sickness."

"I'm with you," Tre said.

I grabbed my 9mm off the dresser, along with my truck keys. We walked in the courtway. I saw the dope fiends and crackheads running around, and kids playing in the courtway.

A couple crackhead come up to me. "Slim, you straight?" they asked.

"No, my nigga got it." I watched as Tre served them. We jumped in my 1991 fairly used black Pathfinder with dark tinted windows and black rims.

I pulled up in the St. Thomas in the 10th Ward. St. Thomas was the third biggest project in the city. This motherfucker project here is real cut-throat. Every nigga that was a killer in the city get found dead back here. These niggas don't fuck around. I don't real give a fuck about these niggas. Fuck them! Fuck these dog ass hoes back here. Them bitch suck all niggas' ass and everything. But them hoes will set you up for a nigga back here. I don't trust them. These hoes ain't shit.

I stepped out the car with my strap on my waist. I walked into the St. Mary Courtway, looking for this nigga—Fee.

The St. Thomas had some fire heroin back here. It was called 911 because every time a nigga hit it, there was call to 911 from a nigga or a hoe concerning a motherfucker who OD'd. They had everybody from all over the city coming back here. Fee dope bags was flooded, and the dope was damn good.

I spotted Fee standing in the hallway. Fee was short, black and bald-headed. This nigga got a fuck up attitude because he on top. He think because a nigga get loaded, he can handle a nigga any kind of way. I real be wanting to jack his fake ass.

If I catch him slipping, I'm going to fuck over him.

"What's up, Fee?" I said.

"What's up, Slim."

"I need a gram of dope and coke."

"Okay."

I watched as he went under the step and grabbed the brown bags. I looked around to see if I could jack his pussy ass. This nigga keeps about at least a couple of ounces dope and coke on him, along with a couple grand in his pocket.

As I walked in the hallway, I drew down my gun on him. "Nigga, let me get everything."

"What the fuck you doing?"

"Nigga, empty your motherfucking pocket."

"Nigga, this shit not going to end well for you."

"Nigga, you threatening me?"

"Take how you want it. You not going to make it out this projects."

"In that case fuck you. I'm going to take you with me." I shot the nigga twice in the chest. Then I broke out running to the truck with sweat on my face.

As I reached the truck, niggas went to shooting. Tre and I hit back. Tre jumped in the driver side as I jumped in the truck, then he pulled off. Them niggas shot out my back glass.

"Shit! Slim. You ain't told me earlier you was going to jack the nigga."

"Fuck the old bitch ass. Nigga, I ain't like him anyway.
"You killed him."
"Yea."
"Shit! That mean war time."
"Fuck them niggas and him."
"You know I don't care. Fuck them."
"I got a couple ounces of dope and coke. And a few stacks.
"Cool with me."
"You know. I'm wild Magnolia."
"I dig."

***

When we walked through the cut in the 6 Court, police thronged the entire place, with yellow and red tape everywhere, a white sheet covering a body. "What the fuck!" I said.

"Nigga got smoke," Tre said. Dime and Bell came walking up to me. They were a couple hood rats out the projects who fuck everybody back here and know everybody business.

"Man, they killed Gee."

"Who?" I asked.

"Niggas out the Melp projects came running back here with AK-47s."

"Damn!"

Gee was a O.G out the circle. He raised me too. But he was on jacking shit like me. He jacked one of the big-time drug dealer who be running the projects. He tied the nigga old lady up and took five bricks of coke.

"Damn! They caught him slipping," Tre said.

We sat in my room, counting the money and snorting coke and dope. It was four grand and five thousand dollars' worth of dope and coke bags. We split the money and drugs.

"Man, I'm out," Tre said.

"Later." I laid back, enjoying my high, smoking a blunt.

Just then I heard a knock at the door. I grabbed my strap, walking to it. "Who is it?"

"Kim."

I opened the door. She walked in wearing her white pants and pink shirt—Her nurse uniform. She worked at Charity Hospital. I met her in the mall one day while she was window-shopping. Kim was older than me. She was twenty-four. I was just seventeen.

"How are you doing?" I said.

"Not good," Kim said.

"Why?"

Looking me square in the eye, Kim stripped down to her bra and panties without ceremony. "I've been horny and dying for a fuck."

There and then I peeled off my clothes while she removed her bra and panties. She jumped into my arms, and I carried her to the bed, where she spread her legs in her eagerness to give me her pussy. I lost no time in entering her sweet spot, her pussy welcoming my thrusts slickly.

The deeper I went in her, slamming my dick up against her pussy walls, the more she cried out.

"I'm coming right there." Her body began to shake as she came all over my dick.

I flipped her over, gripping her ass cheeks, thrusting in and out of her. As she grabbed the sheet, screaming my name, her face pressed against the pillow.

"Fuck! Slim. Fuck! Oh my gosh! You killed me."

I grabbed her by the shoulders, slamming my dick harder and deeper into her. "I'm coming again, don't stop," she said, shaking in a frenzy.

I fucked the shit out of her for about forty-five minutes straight. "I'm about to nut," I said, gripping her ass.

"Damn! Nigga, about time," she said, backing up on me.

I gripped her ass, slid my dick all the way into her as I shot my hot cum deep inside. I laid back on the bed as she grabbed her clothes, putting them on, trying to catch her breath at the same time. "Where you going?"

"Back to work "

"A'ight."

"I'm going to get up with you later, thanks for the nut." She kissed me and walked out the room.

I laid back on the bed, hitting the blunt again"

She my main girl. I fucked her the next night after we first met. She fell in love with me after I fucked her with that dope dick, which had her coming back to back. She's from Slidell—a small city in the outskirt of New Orleans. Her people have money and hate the fact that she's in love with a nigga like me. They told her several times to leave me.

But her ass ain't going nowhere. That dick got her mind gone. Every time she thinking about leaving me or threatening to leave, I tell her ass to go. But she always say she not going to let them hoes win. She a fine yellow bone. She favored Keri Hilson from head to toe. Her ass crazy as a motherfucker, always ready to fight hoes over me. She had two miscarriages for me and she blamed it all on me. She say I stress her out worrying about me in the streets, because she know all the beef shit I got going on. Plus she know I be jacking these fuck niggas out here.

The reason why she my main girl is because I can count on her.

"What's good?" I asked. This was the following day after I had fucked her at my place before she went to work.

"Nigga, I need some dick. Why you ain't answer your phone last night?"

"I was high."

"No. Your ass probably fucking these nasty ass hoes back here. I'm not expecting no baby. I'ma tell you this now, nigga. I need to be the first bitch with your kid."

I followed her to the room. She dropped her pants and panties, getting in the bed, spreading her legs. I climbed in between her, sliding my dick into her soaking wet pussy. I thrust in and out of her, as she dug her nails into my back, telling me how much she loved me.

"Slim, I swear I love you, baby."

Chapter 2

Slim

I stepped out the truck at this club called *49ers*. It's where all the local and underground rappers in the city come to perform. It's around the corner from the Melp projects. I walked in the club, and UNLV was just getting off the mic: They were a hot group under Cash Money Records. They had the underground scene on lock. I was cool with them. I dapped them off as I took the mic. The DJ dropped the track, and I went to rocking my new single: *Shake, Wash, Dush It*. Them hoes was twerking on the dance floor in some shorts and thongs.

I rocked the club for about an hour straight. I had them hoes sweating out their weaves and perms. When I stepped off the stage, niggas went to give me dapps, and hoes went to giving me hugs.

Presently, I was sitting at the bar talking to this red bone with long red weave in her hair. She wore white shorts, red shirt, and white Reebok sneakers. "So what we doing tonight? We fucking?" I asked.

"I'm about whatever you 'bout," she said,

Just then some niggas went to shooting in the club. I grabbed her, falling to the floor. I looked up and saw them niggas out the Melp with hand guns shooting inside the club. I raised up with my gun, shooting along with Tre.

We exchanged gunfire for about five minutes until the police showed up. All of us involved in the shooting broke out running to our cars and jumped in, pulling off.

We sat on the porch in the Magnolia, hitting the blunt. "Man, them niggas almost fuck us up," Tre said.

"I know," I replied. After blowing out a heavy cloud of smoke through my mouth and nostrils, I smiled and added: "It's cool, though."

"It's war time for real," Tre said.

I nodded. "You can say that again, bruh."

***

Two days later, I was riding around the city with my Glock on my lap, looking for a lick to hit. My pocket was hurting. I had snorted the last bag of dope. I was sick with this money on my back. I needed to pull off a stunt that would make me some bread. But I still hadn't come through on the fucking lick yet.

As I rode through uptown, I came through this neighborhood in the 17th Ward in the P-town. Niggas was shooting dice on the block, and it look like they had a nice bit of change on the ground.

I parked a couple cars down, put my black bandanna around my face along with my hat. I jumped out the truck with my gun clocked back, ready to bust if these niggas get to tripping.

I ran up on them, waving my gun at them. "Niggas, this a robbery. Don't make it a murder scene. All you motherfuckers, lay on the ground." It was four of them. I went through their pockets, taking money and guns off them. Then I picked the money up off the ground.

I ran back to my truck, pulling off.

I walked up to this nigga—Joe—in my projects who be selling dope. He stayed at Lasalle on the other side of the project. I really don't like getting done out my projects, because the bag be small and the dope be shitty sometimes.

But right now I don't have choice because I need to get this money off my back.

"Look out, Joel. I need to get a gram."

"Okay." He pulled the plastic bag from under the step, pulling out a gram of dope.

I handed him three hundred dollars.

I sat in my room, hitting line after line along with a line of coke. This was cool, but not like that dope in the St. Thomas. But I couldn't go back there. I know what I could do.

I picked up my cell phone, and called my little bitch who was where she be hustling weed

"Hello," she said.

"I need you do me a favor."

"What you need, nigga?"

"Go in the St. Thomas and get me a gram of dope."

"Nigga, you tripping."

"That's how you going to do me?"

"What you going to give me?"

"Some dick."

"Yea, 'cause you been dragging a bitch. I should let that bitch Kim go get it, since you fucking her."

"Man, chill the fuck out."

"Yea, give me fifteen minutes."

"Okay."

"And I want my money too."

"I got you."

Fifteen minutes later, she was knocking at my door. I opened it up, letting her in. Tracy was my other hoe I was fucking. She was from out of Kenner on the outskirt of the city. She was brown-skinned, thick, with short reddish hair, and a fat round ass that she loved getting fucked in. She was a freak who loved swallowing the come and everything, with tattoos all over her. She had on a pink wife-beater, blue shorts, and black Nike Air Max shoes.

"You got it?"

"Yea, where my money?"

"That's how it is?"

"This was three hundred."

We walked into the room. I gave her three hundred dollars. She reached in the ashtray, grabbing the blunt and hitting it.

As I was snorting the line of dope, she unzipped my pants and pulled out my dick. She went to sucking on it. I laid back, letting her do her thing. She deep-throat like a porn star. She spit on all over my dick, sucking on my balls, making it nasty. She rose up, getting out of her clothes, climbing on top of me, and began riding my dick.

I gripped her ass cheeks so tight, bouncing her hard up and down on my rock-hard dick. She grabbed on her hard brown nipples, biting her bottom lips. I grabbed her shoulders, slamming my dick in out of her soaking wet pussy, as I used my my thumb to finger-fuck her asshole that was wet like her pussy.

She pulled my dick out her pussy, and slid it into her asshole, slamming back on my dick,

"Fuck! Baby, it's good. Fuck me," she said, as she played with her pussy.

I gave it to her just like she loved it—Hard and fast! She shook, climaxing back to back.

I began shaking. "I'm about to nut," I groaned.

She pulled it out her ass, and put it in her mouth, sucking it until I came all in her mouth.

"Hmmm! Baby, you taste good." She licked all of the nut off my dick.

"You a beast," I said, lying back on the bed as she sucked my dick, trying to get back hard.

Later on that night, my phone rang. I looked over at her sleeping next to me.

"Woo Na," I said.

"You going to come lay some raps down?" DJ Mike said.

"Yea, I'm on my way." I looked at the clock. It was 10 p.m.

I jumped in the shower. I got out a few moments after, threw on some black jeans, blue polo shirt, and some black Reeboks. I grabbed my strap along with my blunt and headed out the door.

I walked in the studio. Yellow Boy from the group named UNLV was there along with DJ Mike and this nigga named Bond. DJ Mike was the nigga that put me on when he heard me rapping in the Magnolia. He been helping me getting featured in tracks with other rappers in the city. On his different mix tapes he was always dropping smash hits. DJ Mike was a slim bald head black nigga. Bond was managing different niggas in the city rap scene. He tried to come holler at me. I told him I was cool. I needed all my money from my shows.

Yellow Boy was a hot rapper with the hot group UNLV. We was going to lay some raps down together over this track DJ Mike had made. Yellow Boy was a high yellow nigga with tattoos all over him and a mouth full of golds. As soon as I get my money right I'm going to go get me some.

"You ready?" DJ Mike asked.

"Let do this," I said.

We laid the verses down, then we sat there talking and smoking on a blunt.

"Nigga, I need to hit a lick."

"What you talking?" Yellow said.

"Shit, at least a couple bricks."

"I might got something."

"I'm down."

"A'ight. I'm going to hit up in a little bit. I need some money too." He dapped me off, walking out.

***

We pulled up to this green and white house in the 6th Ward. "Man, look, this a 24/7 power shop. I know they got at least two bricks in there and about fifty grand."

"How you know?"

"I know the nigga brother. He's a big fish down here."

"Okay, let's do it."

We put on our ski mask and stepped out the car with our gun drawn. We ran up the house, kicking in the door. I shot the first nigga at the door.

Yellow ran behind the other nigga, putting the gun to his head. "Nigga, where the money and dope at?"

"Man, please."

I searched the kitchen and found a key in the tide box. "Jackpot."

"Where the keys?"

"Please, man."

I searched the rest of the house, found another key of coke and fifty grand.

Yellow shot the nigga in the head. We ran to the car, jumping in and smashing out.

Later, we sat in Yellow's kitchen, breaking everything up and splitting it down the middle. I took a brick and twenty-five grand. "Later, my nigga, I'm out," I said, dapping him off.

I went home, stashed the coke in my closet and put the money underneath some clothes in my drawer. Tracy ass was gone when I came back.

Next morning, I walked in my mother's room and handed her five grand.

"Slim, where did you get this from?"

"Mom, don't ask questions. Just go buy yourself something nice."

I know my dog was going to be mad with me, because I didn't take him on the lick. But I'm going to pop him off.

As soon as I walked outside into the courtway, his ass was walking up to me.

"Hey, nigga, why you ain't take me on the fucking lick? I thought I was your dog."

"Nigga, you is. And it wasn't my lick I got, though."

"Nigga, where you about to go?"

"First and Claiborne. To get me a mouth full."

"Nigga, I want some too."

"I got you, let's go."

He was my dog. I couldn't leave him hanging.

First and Claiborne is a dentist's office that do everybody's golds in the city. It was right down the street from the Magnolia. It was a small brown brick building in the middle of the block. We walked in. The next thing you know, we were walking out of there with a mouth full of golds. I paid $3400 for both of us.

Back in the Project, they had DJ in the circle. Hoes and niggas from all over was back here. Hoes was shaking their ass to the bounce music. Niggas was standing around strapped, watching the hoes.

As I was coolin' on the steps, talking to Tre, this old fine bitch named Len walked up. She been on my dick for a while but I wasn't trying to give her no play. All she fuck with is young thug-out niggas.

"What's up, Slim?" she said.

"Coolin'. What's good?"

"Let me holla at you."

"I'ma be right back," I said to Tre. He nodded as I got up and followed Len.

Len was black as midnight, about 5'5 with smooth skin, a big ass and thick frame with tattoos of some nigga's name on her neck. She wore her black hair short. She was a straight Magnolia Project 6 Court hoe. She got two kids that stay with her mother in the eastern part of New Orleans. She'd been in and out of jail for stealing out of stores and selling drugs.

"I like the golds you got."

"That what you want to holla at me about?"

"You know a bitch been trying to holla at you. When you going to give some of that fire dick I been hearing about?"

"Holla at me later."

"Don't be playing with me."

"I got you." I watched as she walked off with them little gray shorts that her ass was eating up. She looked back at me, smiling.

"What she was talking about?" Tre asked.

"Me fucking her."

"Nigga, you should have fucked that hoe already. She been on your dick."

"Don't trip, my nigga. I got her."

***

Tre and I sat in the house of this crackhead named Joyce, watching her cook up a half key. I gave Tre nine ounces and took nine ounces. The rest of the key—I left in powder.

"Here y'all go." She dropped the ounces on the table. We cut them up to 25, 50 and 100 slabs. Big ten rocks too.

Moments later, I sat on Len's porch, loaded, ducking off dope with my gun in my lap.

"Slim, you got something?" a crackhead asked.

"Yea, what you need?"

"Three dimes."

"Here you go."

She handed me the money and walked off.

Len walked outside, smoking on a cigarette. She sat next to me on the step with some small red shorts, white wife beater and pink house slippers. "What's up, Slim?"

"Nothing, coolin'. What's good?"

"Need to come inside but you out here ducking when you know full well you got beef."

"Shit! I'm good. I got my gun."

"Slim, let me get two dimes," another crackhead said.

"Here," I said, handing him two as he handed me my money.

"Come on, Slim, let's go inside."

I got up, following her inside. We sat on her couch, smoking a blunt.

She reached over, grabbing my dick. She stroked through my pants as it got hard.

She went down, unzipping my pants, and started sucking my dick.

I laid back, enjoying her sucking my dick.

She rose up, took my hand, leading me to her bedroom. She took off my clothes and pushed me on the bed. She removed her clothes, climbing on top of me, sliding my dick in her wet pussy, and began riding my hard dick.

I grabbed her ass cheeks, spreading them, slamming her down on my dick as she screamed out my name and dug her nails in my chest.

"Fuck! Slim, this dick is good. I'm about to come already." Her body shook, and she was coming all over my dick with her eyes rolling in the back of her head.

I flipped her over, slamming my dick in and out of her as she gripped the sheet, screaming my name. "Fuck! Fuck! Slim! You killing me."

"Bitch! Shut up and take this dick. This what you want, huh?"

She tried to run from this dick. I gripped her ass cheeks,

pulling her, thrusting in and out of her, and she screamed my name.

"Slim! I—I—I'm coming," she stuttered out, shaking.

I flipped back over, pulling her legs on my shoulders, busting her out.

"Fuck! Slim, I feel you all in my stomach."

I began to shake. "Fuck! I'm coming," I said, shooting all my hot nut in her pussy.

"Yes, babe, shoot that nut all in this pussy. This your pussy."

I laid next to her, trying to catch my breath.

Robert Baptiste

Chapter 3

Slim

Next morning, while I was on the porch trying to catch the early morning rush, serving crackheads, Tre walked up to me, smoking on a blunt.

"What's up, man?" He dapped me off.

"Nothing, just catching this morning rush," I said.

Len walked outside wearing some purple shorts, shirt to match and house slippers.

"Babe, you want something to eat?"

"Nah, I'm good."

"I see you smashed," Tre said in a whisper.

"I told you I would," I replied.

Len walked inside.

"Was it good?" said Tre.

"She can't take no dick. I put that dope dick on her ass and had her running. I know that what them hoes want."

"Here, Slim," Len said as she emerged.

"Where mine?" said Tre, looking from my grits and cheese to Len.

"I'm not fucking you. You not my man."

"Give my partner some of them grits and cheese."

"Boy—"

"Bitch! Go get that shit."

"Who you calling a bitch?"

"I gotta roll, my nigga," Tre said.

"Oh. Well, I'ma about go get in the shower. I'm going to catch up with you later."

"Okay, later." Tre left, pronto.

I walked off, brushing past Len as I went inside, not even looking back.

"So that's how it is?" she said, but I kept mute, making my way to the bathroom.

I stepped out the shower once I was done, and walked in the

room. I put on my gray Girbaud, gray wife-beater, along with some gray Reeboks, and draped the polo over my shoulders. I grabbed five stacks and my pistol, walking out the house.

I stopped at the Western Union, sending my brother five hundred dollars.

I watched as they fixed the truck window. I pulled off and rode around to the parkway. I fucked with a few niggas over there. It was a small little hood down the streets from the Magnolia. I pulled up on this nigga—Dee—who I know from joshing in back town.

For the record, joshing means doing time. We did a few months in the H.O.D. I was in there fighting a drug charge that I eventually beat. He was in there on one too. We got cool. And we been hanging ever since.

I stepped out the truck, walking up to him. "What's up, nigga"

"What's up, man?" I said, dapping him off.

Dee was short, about 5'4, brown-skinned and with a bald head. He had on some green Levis with a white wife-beater, and black Reeboks, along with a big .45 on him

"Shit, nigga out here getting my hustle. And you?"

"Just coming through coolin'." I sat there talking to him for a couple minutes. I really didn't like being around there because them white folk be hot around there.

"Man, I'm out."

"Later," he said, dapping me off.

As I was about to head back to the Magnolia, I saw a police car pulling up behind me.

"Man, I sure don't need these dick suckers fucking with me," I said to myself. As I was about to cross over Claiborne, the police hit the lights. "Fuck!" I said, pulling over.

I slid the gun under the seat. It was this motherfucker named Sgt. Branson. A white man with blonde hair. This motherfucker be on my dick all the time. He's the reason why I was fighting a drug charge back town. The white motherfucker was a racist piece of shit. Always fucking with a nigga,

He stepped out the police car, wearing a dark blue police

uniform. He walked up to my truck with his gun drawn. I pulled my window down.

I know this bitch was going to fuck with me because my truck smelled just like a pound of weed. "Why the fuck you coming up to my truck with your gun out!" I said, showing him my mouth full of golds.

"Get the fuck out the truck!"

"Man, fuck you! Pulling your gun out on a traffic stop makes no goddamn sense."

"Get the fuck out the truck."

Just then, some more police cars pulled up and a few officers stepped out their cars, walking over to my truck. "What's going on?" they asked.

"This asshole don't want to get out the truck."

"Sir, just step out the truck."

"Fuck that racist piece shit, pulling his gun on for a traffic stop."

"Sir, just step out."

I stepped out the truck and soon Sgt. Branson put his gun up. Pouncing on him, I hit him right in the eye. We got to wrestling. The other police officers broke us up. They placed me in handcuffs, reading my right, placing me in the back of the police car.

They drove me to Central Lockup back of town.

They walked me into Central Lockup where the C.O. processed me on battery charges on the police. "What's my charge?" I asked.

"Battery." She took my hand and pressed it on the ink, taking my finger prints. She gave me an orange band.

In the jail, there were different kinds of bands for the charges you were on. Red bands mean capital offense, orange bands range from crime-related offenses to drugs, weapons or battery, and yellow mean misdemeanor.

The chubby, dark-skinned woman with blonde hair walked to the hold tank which was nasty with all kinds of writing scribbled on the wall, and a toilet that reeked of piss. It was about ten niggas in there, and only one phone. I needed to make a phone call and bond out this shit. I know this bitch took my truck to the pound. I hope them bitches didn't find my gun.

As I was about to make a call, the chubby lady opened the door, calling my name.

"Hey, what good?" I said to her.

"Come, you going upstairs."

A black male C.O. took me to the back. Where he made me strip, spread my ass cheeks and cough and lift up my feet. He handed me an orange jump suit. He then gave me a blanket, cup and toothpaste.

The C.O. took me upstairs to H.O.D. In this motherfucker you can't be no hoe. You got to be about your business. I been in H.O.D for the gun charges. H.O.D stands for House of Detention. The C.O. will fuck you up in here. It had four dorms on each floor. But you got to be from the right spot or niggas will jump up if you're not from there. If you're from Uptown, that's the dorm you need to be in; but if you're from Downtown, that's where you need to be at.

I stepped out of the elevator on the 6th floor. They opened the iron door. I walked on the tier. It was three cells with twelve people in each one of them. They stay shutdown. They got one two phones. Niggas be trying to hog it if they thinking you a hoe. You get one hour of rec yard.

When I walked in the cell, I saw a few niggas I know from the projects. "What's up, Slim?" Lil' Dee and Mel said.

"Nothing. What's up, Dee and Mel?"

Dee was a short, brown-skinned nigga with a bald head. He was in here for a gun charge. Mel was facing a drug charge that bitch Sgt. Branson busted him for. Mel was chubby, dark-skinned with good hair.

"What they got you for?"

"Battery on this bitch sergeant."

"I'm glad you fuck that bitch up."

"Rec yard," the C.O said. "You going?"

"Yea."

As I walked in the hallway, I saw a couple of niggas out the St. Thomas. The niggas were boothing me up.

"Nigga, who the fuck you boothing up?" I asked them.

"You, nigga."

I rushed over to them nigga, throwing fists. We went in the mix, fighting

Then the other homeboy of one of the niggas jumped in, and my homeboy jumped in. It turned out to be a big gang fight. The C.O. ran in, spraying pepper spray. That shit went to blind all of us. The rest of the police broke us up. They had us on our stomach, handcuffed with our face full of blood and spray.

The captain walked on the floor. He was an old black man with gray hair, and walked with a cane. His name was Captain Williams.

"What that fuck was this shit about?" he said, smoking on a cigarette.

"This bitch ass nigga killed my homeboy," one of the nigga's said, pointing at me.

"Well, you motherfucker niggas had better be friends in this motherfucker, or all you bitches will be in the fucking hole." Facing the C.O., the captain said, "Put this motherfuckers back on the tier, ain't no rec, phone and TV."

We went back on the tier, and the C.O. locked all the cells.

"Man, what that shit was about?" Dee asked.

"I smoked their homeboy sometime ago."

"Fuck them niggas."

"Yea, fuck them. I need to use the phone though." I walked over to the phone, using it before they cut it off.

"Hello."

"Yea."

"Mom, what they talking?"

"You go to court in the morning."

"Okay, they about to cut the phone off. Because I just got in a fight."

"For what?" she asked.

"I can't tell you that on the phone."

"Okay, just know you go to court in the morning."
"Okay, I love you."
"Love you."
"Wait, what they said about my truck?"
"Four hundred to get out the pound."
"Okay." I hung up the phone, getting in line to eat the food.

***

Next morning, about 7:00 a.m., the C.O. walked on the tier, calling my name. "Morris Brown, pack your shit. Court."
I grabbed my shit and dapped my niggas off. "Man, y'all be cool. I'll see you niggas on the other side."
"Love, nigga."
"Later."
The chubby fat lady with gold hair was waiting on at the iron black bars. I walked outside; she patted me down and put shackles and handcuffs on me. Then she walked me to the white van.
I saw a couple people from around my way. They were going to court too. Among them were Tamika and Cindy from off second streets. These hoes be stealing and setting niggas up. I fucked both of them back in the game. Tamika was high yellow with red hair and tattoos all over her body. Cindy was light brown, pie-faced, big-assed and ugly.
"What y'all in here for?" I asked.
"Stealing clothes."
"What they talking?"
"Two years."
"I hear y'all."
"You know I'm going to need some of that dope dick when I come home," Cindy said.
"You better know it. You been acting fun with the dick."
"I see you got a mouth full of golds."
"You know how I do it."
"What you in for?"
"Battery on Sergeant's pussy ass."

"Fuck that hoe," Cindy said.

"You already know."

"Let's go," the C.O said.

"Y'all be cool," I said.

"You too, Slim, see you when we get out."

I walked behind the old parish jail. That's where the courtroom is located. The place was nasty with trash everywhere, writings on the wall and all these colors of paint peeling off the wall. It had three holding cells that were filling with niggas sleeping and sitting on benches, waiting to go to court.

I walked in and dapped a few niggas off I knew. Niggas were from all different parts of the jail.

I sat on the bench, waiting for my name to be called. A couple minutes later, a white public defender came calling my name. "Morris Brown."

"Here," I said, standing up.

He was short with blond hair, and wore a brown suit and penny loafers. My name is Chad Stevenson. I'm going be representing you."

"Okay, what's up?"

"Well, today you going to take a plea and one year probation. And you free."

"Okay, cool. When do I get in court?"

"Just a minute."

In the courtroom I stood next to the public defender, listening to the judge speak. "Mr. Brown, I see you took a plea."

"Yes, Your Honor."

"Okay, well, I'm going to honor that plea and give you one year probation."

"Okay, thank you."

"Mr. Brown, keep your hands off the police. Or next time you will be serving time."

"Okay, thanks."

***

At home, I jumped out the shower, drying off. I walked in the room and grabbed a foil pack, snorting it to get the tension off my back. Then I grabbed the weed and put it inside of the cigar, rolling it up. I grabbed the lighter, firing it up. I took a couple puffs and blew the smoke out of my nose and mouth.

I put on some black Girbauds, white wife beater and black Reeboks.

I draped a red polo shirt over my shoulders, and grabbed the .45 pistol out the clothes, stuffed it in my waist line along with a couple stacks, and walked out the house with my girl. "I need to go to the pound and get my truck," I said.

"A'ight, I'm going with you," she replied, as I hailed a cab.

"Okay."

I asked the cabby to pull up to the pound across the street for the Iberville Projects in the 4th Ward downtown across the streets from the graveyard. My girl waited outside as I walked up the window. A chubby red chick with red hair was working.

"Yes, can I help you?"

"Yea, I'm trying to get my truck."

"License."

"In my truck."

"What it look like?"

"Black Pathfinder."

"Okay." She looked up on her computer. "Yes, follow me."

I followed behind her as she walked me to my truck. I was just hoping my gun was still there.

I opened the door, feeling under the seat. It was still there.

"Here, my license and registration." I handed it to her.

"It going to be four hundred—"

"Okay."

After I had the whole thing sorted out, I kissed my girl and pulled off with her in the passenger side of my truck.

***

Later that night, I sat on the porch, serving rocks, smoking a blunt.

I spotted this fat ass nigga named Burger out the Melp creeping out the house of this bitch named Pat. This nigga got balls coming back here after they killed Gee. *I got his ass.* I picked the Glock off my lap.

As he was coming out the hallway, I ran up on him. "What's up, nigga?" I let him have it. I shot him five times in the chest. Then I stood over him, letting him have it. I emptied the click into his face. Then I broke out running. I ran to Len's house and knocked on the door. She opened up, wearing green shorts, white wife beater, smoking a blunt"

"Slim, what wrong? Why you sweating?"

I pushed past her. "Here, put this up."

She grabbed the strap and ran to the back room.

I sat on the couch, nervous. I picked the blunt out the ashtray, hitting it.

She walked back in the living room, looking nervous as me. "Was that you shooting?"

"Yea,"

"Shit. You killed him."

"Go look out the window and see what you can see."

"Shit! They got the police out here. They got the whole courtway blocked off, with a white sheet covering up a body."

"Damn!"

"Don't trip if they come asking questions—I got you—You been fucking me all night," she said, hitting the blunt, blowing smoke out her nose.

Robert Baptiste

Chapter 4

Slim

"Shit! This dope fire," I said, leaning my head back on the head rest in Tre's car.

"You know them niggas out the St. Thomas still looking to kill you, huh? They heard you home," Tre said.

"Man, fuck them niggas."

"That nigga Wayne got ten grand on your head."

Wayne was June's big brother. June was the nigga I killed. Wayne ran shit back there in the St. Thomas. He gave them niggas all the dope. He got a connect in New York.

"Fuck that fuck nigga! I'm thinking about jacking his pussy ass anyway."

"Let me know when you ready."

"I got you. What up with this lick tonight?" I asked, snorting another line.

"Nigga, it in the eight ward. This nigga leaves brick by his babymother's house."

"About how many?"

"Two or three for sure."

"What kind of money?"

"Like fifty thousand."

"How you know?"

"I been fucking the big Les on the cool. And she been poppin' me off cool, talking the nigga business."

"A'ight, it's game on!"

When we pulled up at this red brick house on the corner on St. Rock across the street from the park, we jumped out with guns in our hands and ran up to the door, kicking it in. A fat light-skinned woman got up from the couch, screaming with her kids, trying to run. I grabbed the bitch by her head and dragged her to the bedroom.

"Check the house," I said.

"I'm on it."

"Bitch! Where the dope and money at?" I said, throwing her ass on the bed.

"I swear I don't know what you talking about."

"I'm going to ask you one last time, bitch! Don't fuck with me."

"Please don't kill me. I have two kids."

"Well, bitch, you need to start talking."

"Man, I got the keys," Tre hollered out from the kitchen.

"Bitch! Where the fucking money?"

"In the clothes."

"Thank you, bitch!" I said, shooting her in the head.

I went in the clothes, searching it. I came up to a couple of shoe boxes with rolls of money. I grabbed it. Tre ran in the room with the two key in his hands.

"Man, what the fuck is going on? Why you shoot the bitch?"

"Fuck you mean? This bitch seen our face. I'm going down for no murder and armed robbery."

"Come on, nigga. I hear police siren."

"Nigga, where the fucking kids? They got to go too."

"Nigga, fuck that shit, we got to go." Tre ran out the house. I looked around for the little boys. But the police siren was getting close. I ran out the house, jumped in the car as he smashed out.

"So you really were gonna shoot those kids!" Tre said, shaking his head in disbelief. "My nigga, you tripping," he added.

***

We sat in my mother's kitchen, splitting the key and money up. It was fifty thousand in cash.

"Man, it was a nice lick," I said, hitting the blunt.

"For sure," Tre said, hitting his blunt.

"I need to get back on my feet." I blew the smoke out my nose.

"Shit, me too."

Between the dope and the weed, I felt off. "I'm with you. I'ma trade my truck in and go get another one. That motherfucker too hot."

"I feel you. I'm about to get me a ride too because my shit hot too from all the robbing and jacking I do. A nigga can easily kill me through my car."

"Shit! I can't even creep down on a nigga if I want to because niggas know my truck."

"Shit, I'm out."

"Nigga, you be cool."

"Oh, shit straight on that murder shit, huh?"

"Yea, you know the hood not talking. You know I had to get that nigga for the hood. Fuck them niggas out the Melp. They think we pussy, but we will show them."

"I feel you represent for the Wild Magnolia. I'm out."

"Be cool." I dapped him off.

I grabbed my stuff, brought them to my bed. I stacked them in the bottom drawer and put the money up. I laid across my bed, feeling high, then I fell asleep.

The next morning, I got up, took a shower. I got out dressed in blue Girbauds, black and red polo, and Reeboks. I grabbed my gun, put it in my waist. I grabbed twenty thousand grand, and walked into the living room. My mother was sitting on the couch, watching TV.

"Here, momma, ten grand to pay the bills and the rest of which I need to hire a lawyer down the line."

"You be safe in them fucking streets."

"You know I got this," I said, kissing her on the cheeks.

I walked outside, looking for Mark. Mark was an O.G nigga that sold dope. It was cool but not that fire, though I needed to kill that morning sickness. I spotted him in the courtway serving. I walked up to him.

"What's up, Slim ?"

"I need two bags," I said, pulling out fifty dollars.

"Here."

I took the two bags, snorting them as I walked through the cut, headed to my truck. I hopped in and put the gun on my lap, pulling off.

I made my way to this used car lot on Canal St. I had been seen this black Explorer. It was fairly used, a 1993 model for $17,500. I was going to try and talk that motherfucker into letting me trade my truck in and get it for twelve grand.

As soon as I walked on the lot, a black fat guy with nappy hair and beard came out wearing an old brown suit with a white button down shirt.

"Yes, can I help you?"

"Ya, I want to cop this Explorer."

"Okay." He opened it up for me. It had black leather seat, and was plain on the inside.

"How many people had it?"

"Three."

"How many mile?"

"Ten thousand."

"Okay, I'll take it, but I want to trade it in for my truck and give you twelve thousand grand."

"I need seventeen thousand five hundred dollars"

"I got twelve thousand cash right now."

"Right now?"

"Ya."

"Okay, you got a deal. Let's go do the paper work."

An hour later, I drove off the lot. I pulled up to Motor One in the eastern part of New Orleans, and got them to put 12-inch woofers in the back, and 6 by 9 speakers in the doors.

I pulled off, blasting 2Pac—one of my favorite rappers. I took the car to get washed, then I pulled up in the Magnolia on the set and opened the door, playing bounce music for the juveniles in my hood. The girls among them were shaking their asses.

Tre pulled up in a Buick, blasting Eric B. and Rankim.

"Nigga, I see you cop a whip."

"I told you I was going to do it."

"See you got a new truck."

"You understand me."

Thirty minutes later, we were in the middle of the Circle, smoking weed and getting high off heroin, selling rocks and powder bags.

Robert Baptiste

Chapter 5

Slim

It had been a couple of weeks since I killed that fat motherfucker—Burger. That nigga must have thought we were hoes back here. He didn't know this was the home of Slim. I was worrying about nobody in the projects because we had a no ratting policy back here.

So I think I'm straight.

As I was smoking on a blunt, writing raps and loaded off dope and coke, I heard the front door come flying open.

I went to grab my gun. But the NOPD bust in my room, pointing their guns and showing me their badges.

"Get the fuck on the ground now, motherfucker," they said.

I got down on the bed as they rushed me and put handcuffs on me, reading me my rights.

The police officers walked me to the living as the rest of them reached the apartment.

Just then, Sergeant Branson walked in the apartment. "I got your ass now, motherfucker," he said, showing me the warrant.

"You ain't got shit on me, motherfucker, fuck you."

He just smiled.

"I want my lawyer."

"You going to need one."

The other police came from the back with my .45 in a plastic bag. "Is that the gun?" the sergeant asked.

"We let you know when we bring it to the lab."

"Okay, get his black ass outta here."

The police put me in the back of the car, and pulled off.

***

The police walked me into Central Lockup.

As the light-skinned slim chick with red hair processed me in, she gave me a red arm band.

"What I'm being charged with?" I asked

"Murder."

"Murder! Y'all tripping. I ain't killed nobody."

"Take that up with the judge."

The black bald head C.O. came over and walked me to the cell. I walked to the phone, and called my girl—Kim.

"Hello."

"I'm in jail."

"For what?"

"Murder."

"Murder! No, Slim!"

"Chill, it's going to be alright."

"You need a lawyer?"

"Yea, I'm going to holler at my mother."

"Okay. Love you."

"Love you back."

I hung up with her and called my mother.

"Hello," she said.

"Ma, I'm in jail."

"I already know. What you in for?"

"Murder."

"Okay, I'm going to try and get you a lawyer."

"Check my room at the bottom of the dresser. I got twenty grand."

"Okay, I got it. I'm going to handle it for you and send you some money."

"Okay, love you."

"Love you."

A few minutes later, the sheriff came and transported me to the Old Parish. The Old Parish was behind the court building. The iron garage raised up as the sheriff drove me in the building. They took me out the car and walked me in the building where the red sign read: YOU ARE NOW ENTERING A REAL JAIL.

The Old Parish has a morgue underneath it where they bring dead bodies to be examined. I heard a story about the Old Parish from O.G niggas that had been up in here. They told how motherfuckers get raped and killed in this motherfucker. And how it has a dark cloud and a dark feeling over it. You got to be a real man in here or niggas was fucked up and killed in here. And the shit you do in here follows you up state.

The Old Parish housed nothing but armed robbers, murderers, rapists, and any other criminals who committed capital offense.

The guard buzzed us in. They walked me past the iron door with the thick window, and walked me into a holding cell that was painted green. A few minutes later, I was stripping butt ass naked, spreading my ass cheeks and coughing and lifting up my feet. The guard handed me an orange jumper. They allowed you to keep your tennis.

The guard handed me a bed roll which consisted of a blanket, cup, toothbrush, and toothpaste. They walked to B1—a locked down unit on the first floor.

It was dark as shit in there. Everybody was sleeping. The iron door slammed behind me; it had me feeling a little nervous. I don't know if I had enemies or not in this tier. I walked to the cell, slammed my mat down on the bunk, and climbed in there falling asleep.

About a couple of hours later, I heard somebody howling and fed up. I got up looking at the chicken wire that separated us from the other side. I put on my tennis and took a piss. I grabbed the tooth brush and tooth paste, brushing my teeth. I walked out the cell, looking at everybody in line waiting to get their plate.

I really wasn't hungry. I was sick. I needed a fix.

I walked back to the cell, going into my tennis, pulled out a gram and snorted me a line.

I walked in line and I saw my nigga—Chill Will— serving the food. Chill was from the Magnolia. But he was from off Lasalle side. He was an O.G in my projects. He was in here on a murder charge. He'd killed a nigga in the mid-city while trying to rob out some keys of coke. He been in here fighting charges like two years now.

"What the fuck deal!" I said, as I dapped him off.

"What's up, Slim? Long time," he said, dapping me.

After he served everybody, he filled my plate up to the top with oat meal and cheese. We sat in the cell, talking, catching up. "What they got you on?" Chill asked.

"Murder in the projects."

"Who?"

"Nigga out the Melp."

"Oh."

"But what's up with you, bitch?"

I went to trial and get two life sentences."

"Damn! My nigga."

"Yea, shit happens."

Just then, a young nigga named Tank from our project came in. "What's up, Slim?"

"Coolin'."

"What they got you on?"

"Body."

"I just beat a body. But the feds picked up my gun case."

"The feds! Good luck with that shit," I replied.

"Morris Brown, get ready for court," the C.O. said across the speaker.

"Fuck with y'all when I get back." I walked to the door as the C.O opened it. Two C.O.'s were waiting on me. They put handcuffs on my hands and shackled my ankles. They walked me down to the nasty ass docks where a nigga had to wait for court.

The docks were behind the court building down the hallway from the old parish. They were nasty with rats and roaches running around everywhere and paint peeling off the walls. Food and trash everywhere with niggas sleeping on the floor and benches in the three holding cells that were made of iron bars.

I went in the cell, laying on the bench, falling asleep. Twenty minutes later, some white man came calling my name. I already knew that the judge probably wouldn't give me bond and if he did, it would probably be too high for me to reach.

"I'm your lawyer. Larry Batiste."

"He was short, bald-headed and looked like a Jew. "Okay."

"They going to pull you out so I can talk to you."

"A'ight."

The C.O. handcuffed me and walked me to the visitation room. I sat across from him as he was looking through some paperwork.

"Okay, I see you being charged with capital murder. Your mother hired me represent you."

"So what you think about bond?"

"Well, to be straight with you, I don't think we're going to get it. But we can try."

"So what they got on me?"

"Well, I just got your case. I got to go over everything. I'll let you know in a couple days."

"Okay."

"Well, today we're just going in there to plead not guilty and see if they're going to give you a bond."

"Okay."

Five minutes later, I walked in the court room, seeing Kim and my mother seated in the court room. People were moving fast, trying to get in their place before the judge came in.

I nodded at Kim and my mom.

The lawyer came and whispered in my ear. "Remember here to plead not guilty."

"Okay."

"All rise. Judge Freeman is presiding."

A white chubby bald head man with a snow-white beard and glasses, wearing a long black robe, came along.

"Mr. Brown, you know what you're being charged with?" the judge asked me.

"Yes, Your Honor, he does," Batiste responded.

"Well, I'm going to let you know anyway. You're being charged with capital murder. Where are we on bond?"

"Your Honor, we feel bond should be denied because this is a capital murder."

"Well, Your Honor, this Mr. Brown's first serious offense."

"He does have a battery on the police officer."

"Okay, enough. Bond set at million dollar cash or property equivalent to the cash. Court adjourned."

I looked at my mother and girl and nodded. "Love y'all," I said to them.

"I'ma come see you in a week," Batiste said.

I walked on the tier, and called my mother on the phone.

"Hello," she said.

"How much you pay for him?"

"Eight thousand five hundred. The rest want thirty grand."

"He good."

"Okay."

"I put money on your books too."

"Okay, love you."

"I'm going to be up there this weekend."

"You don't have to."

"Boy, I'm not trying to hear that. I know what going on in Orleans Parish jails. How them guard be killing people in there. I'll be up there to see your ass."

"Okay, love you."

"Love you too."

I hung up and called my girl.

"What's up, baby?"

"Nothing, wishing you was here."

"Me too."

"I'm going to come and see you Saturday."

"A'ight."

"And I put a hundred dollars on your books."

"Good looking."

"I got you. I'm going to hold you down."

"Love you."

"Love you too."

I got in the shower, thinking about what these bitches could have on me. I know they don't have the exact gun because Len still got it. I know they don't have no witness.

As I was getting dressed, the C.O. called me to the door. I walked to the door. She had a package for me to sign for. In here you can get sheets, towel, PJ's, and slippers. Along with tennis boxes and bandana. "Here, your stuff."

"A'ight." I emptied it on the bed. I had a couple PJ long johns, slippers and tennis, even a gold rag. You can get one of these every week. I shined up my golds, and tied the black bandanna round my neck, walking outside the cell.

I walked into Chill Will's cell, where him and Tank was smoking weed. "Let me hit that?"

"Here." Chill Will passed it to me. "What they said at court?"

"They give me a million dollar bond."

"Well, they know a nigga can pay it."

"What the lawyer talking?" Tank asked

"He said he going to holler at me when he get the paperwork."

"You think that got something on you?"

"I don't see how."

"Man, it like this—If they do try and get a low number, don't let those bitch railroad you and give you life."

"I got you."

***

Tre

I sat on the porch in the Magnolia project, smoking on a blunt, serving rocks load of dope, talking to few of me and Slim niggas.

"Man, they got my guy on murder charges," I said.

"That's fucked up," Free said.

"Yea, but you know how that nigga feels about the project— He rep this motherfucker faithfully," Chad said.

"You already know how I feel about that nigga. Fuck them," I said.

"Tre, you got something?" a crackhead said.

"Yea, what you trying to get?"

"Two dimes."

I pulled out the plastic bag and handed her the dimes. As she gave me the cash, Len walked out on the porch calling my name.

51

"Tre, telephone."

I ran upstairs to her apartment. "What's up?" I said.

"What's good, my nigga?"

"Man, how are you?"

"Man, I'm coolin'. Holding shit down in here."

"What they talking you your case?"

"I'm waiting for the lawyer to come see me. They talking about witness because you know—"

"Chill, you can't talk like that on this phone."

"It all good."

"Man, I'm going to give Len ass a hundred for you."

"Okay, put her back on the phone."

"Love you, my nigga."

"Same here."

"What's up, baby?" Len said.

"I'm good, you?"

"You already know. I'm missing you."

"Miss you too, baby. I gotta go now. Take good care of yourself."

"A'ight, baby. Love you, Slim."

"Same here."

Chapter 6

Slim

"Morris Brown, get ready for visit." I put on my pressed red jump suit with my black Reeboks and shine up my golds. I put on my black bandanna, walking out of my cell.

I walked in the visitation room, walking down the hallway, looking through the glass windows. Some of them was broken and shattered. The visitation room was filthy with nasty writing and peeling off green paint, and cum everywhere.

I found my mother sitting there. I sat down, picking up the phone. "Hey, mom."

"How you holding up in there?"

"I'm good. You know me holding it down like a soulja. How you?"

"You know how it is here paying bills."

"You talking to the lawyer?"

"Yea, he said he going to come see you in a couple days."

"Okay, you talk to my brother."

"Yea, he said if you come that way, he got you."

"Okay, tell him I love him."

"Okay, I put a hundred on your books."

"Thanks, mom, I love you."

"Same here. I'ma go because Kim down stairs waiting to come up."

"Okay."

I watched as she walked the hallway. I could tell she wanted to cry, but held back the tears. I know it hurt her to have two kids in the system. One got life and the other looking at life.

Just then, Kim walked up to the booth wearing tight green jeans, red button down blouse, and black heels. Her hair was pulled back in a ponytail. She smelled so good. He picked up the phone, smiling.

"Hey, baby. How you doing?"

"You know me holding it down like a big dog. You feel me?"

"Yea, baby, I know you holding it down. When they talking about letting you go?"

"I don't know. I haven't talk to the lawyer yet."

"Okay, let me know something."

"You look good. And smell good."

"Thank you. I miss you."

"Miss you too."

She put her hand on the glass, I put mine there too. "I love you," she said.

"Love you too."

While we were talking, she started crying.

"Don't cry, Kim."

"I'm sorry. It's just that I miss you."

"It going to be alright."

"Visitation over!" the C.O. screamed.

"Love you, Slim."

"Love you."

I hung the phone up, and walked back to the dorm. Almost immediately, the C.O. called my name, saying I had a visitor. Kim had already gone, so I wondered who it might be.

When I walked back out there, I didn't see nobody. I walked to the very end, and Len was sitting there with some black tights on that had her pussy showing like a camel toe, and pink halter top and sandals on with her hair hanging. "I thought you said you was coming Sunday."

"I was down this way paying some bills, so I stop through."

"I feel you."

"What's up with you? I put some money on your books."

"Thanks. Well, nothing particularly is up. Just holding down like a dog."

"I know that, right."

"I see you got that pussy out."

"You like?" She smiled, spreading her legs even farther.

"Hell yea." I looked down the hallway. Then I pulled my dick out and jerked off as she watched.

"Damn! Baby, I wish you was here to give some of that."

"Me too," I said, coming all over the floor.

"Visit over."

"Love you, be up here next week."

"Love you too." I watched as she walked down the hallway, twisting with no draws on.

***

Two Weeks Later

Slim

I sat in the visitation booth, listening to the lawyer. "I got the paper work."

"Okay, what it looking like?"

"Well, not good."

"What you mean?"

"Well, the police said they got your finger prints off the shell casing."

"What! They lying."

"The gun they found don't match the shells. That's a good thing."

"Okay, now what?"

"Well, I can get you a lesser charge."

"Man, I need to beat this thing."

"Well, tell me everything that really happened that day."

"Look, I'm not about to talk me business."

"Well, how can I fight it?"

"Look, I give my money. I need you to beat this shit."

"Look, I'm going to shoot straight: if you go to trial the jury going to convict you of murder."

"Man, I could have kept my money and got me a public defender for all this shit. What good are you for?" I got up and walked out, leaving him there.

I walked on the dorm, thinking this whole shit not looking good. I dialed my mother's number.

"Hello. The lawyer came to see you?"

"Yea, and it not looking good."

"What did he say?"

"They got my finger print on the shell casing."

"Damn! Slim! So you tell me I'm going to lose both my kids to the fucking jail system?"

"I don't know yet."

"How much time you looking at?"

"Life."

She started crying.

"I'ma call you back," I said, hanging up.

I called my girl.

"Hello."

"Where you at?"

"At work. What going on?"

"It don't look good."

"What you mean?"

"The lawyer came and seen me today."

"What he talking?"

"They got my finger print on the shell."

"What does that mean?"

"I'm looking at life."

"Life?"

"If I go to trial—"

"Please call me back."

My head started hurting.

I walked to my cell with my head smoking. The feds already came and got Tank and Chill Will waiting to go for that ride to Angola.

I laid in the bed with my head smoking, thinking about what I was going to do.

Later, around four in the morning, Chill Will came to my cell. "Slim, I'm gone."

"What's up?"

"I'm on the bus. You the tier rep now."

"I got out my bed, hugging and dapping him off. "Man, be

cool."

"This all my stuff. And remember what I told you. Don't let them white folk give you a life sentence. Try to get you something you can do. I see you on the river if you come up there. I'm out."

"Later."

***

For the next couple days, I was going back and forward with the lawyer and the prosecutor. I listened to what Chill had told me. I got the lawyer to get the charge broken down to manslaughter. But they offered me fifty years at first. Then came with twenty. I still didn't take it. The next deal the lawyer brought to me was for ten years with no bail. Bail mean if I plead guilty, they could double my time.

I got tired of fighting, so I took the ten. I had been in the parish jail for nine months, and I was tired being in there.

Out of ten years, I could do at least eight and a half or get parole in two years. I could handle that.

I walked in the court room, looked at my mother and girl on the front roll. I stood next to my lawyer as the judge read over the plea agreement which I was to sign.

"Morris Brown, I see you sign a plea today."

"Yes, Your Honor."

"Okay, you sign it because you want to. Nobody forced you, right?"

"Yes, Your Honor."

"You know I don't have to accept this, right?"

"Yes, Your Honor."

"Okay. Well, I'm going to sentence you to ten years in the department of the D.O.C. Court adjourned."

I turned and hugged my mother and Kim.

Robert Baptiste

Chapter 7

Slim

Two weeks later, I was on the white bus headed to Angola. Angola was our maximum prison where they send all the hard criminals to. If your jacket was fucking up, this where you was going. *On the river* is what they called it. Because it sits at the mouth of the Mississippi River.

Now O.G niggas from out the project and from uptown got story about that river, stressing how you got to be a man because niggas was getting stabbed, killed and raped up there.

The prison was filled with Louisiana niggas, dudes from New Orleans, Baton Rouge, Shreveport, and other surrounding areas.

If you pussy, you going to get fucked. Those same rules apply like in the Parish jail. You got to be about your business. Your rep follows. And that not a good look in the hood.

We made it to the front gate; the C.O. let us in. Then we had to go through another iron gate. Then it was a sign that said: *Welcome to Louisiana State Penitentiary.* The penitentiary had the following nicknames: *Angola, Alcatraz of the South,* and *The Farm.* From what I heard, it seemed to be the largest maximum-security prison in the United States with 6,300 prisoners and 1800 staff, including corrections officers, wardens, maintenance, and janitors. It was big. They had houses on the place. People lived there. We rode past different camps until we turned in this dirt parking lot where four different guards were standing wearing black and red uniform with black boots. It was two big country white boys with bald heads and two big country black niggas with bald heads.

And they looked like they did play the radio loud.

When we stepped off the bus, a couple of niggas I came up here with had some scared looks on their faces. Niggas was at the fences, screaming shit at us.

We heard one among them say: "Nigga, don't be scared, you going to be my hoe."

I already had on my mind that the first nigga to play with me would get a full-blown war from me, no question asked. I'm not about to be no nigga hoe or let a nigga get out of line with me. I was a soulja on the streets and in the old parish. I wasn't about to come up here and be a hoe.

"Welcome to Angola," one of the big white boys said. He walked up and down the line, looking at us as he talked. "My name is Captain Darkness. This is my ship. I run it how I want. If you are here, it means you fucked up in the world. So give your soul to God, because your ass is mine. In here, I'm your mother, father, and your lover. You eat, shit and piss when I say so. If you get out of line with my C.O.'s, we going to fuck you up and even might kill you. You can run but you won't get away. There's got a gator farm out there. This is Lt. Edward, C.O. Fore and C.O. Walter. This is the main prison where you sorry motherfuckers are going to be housed. Now move your ass to the shower area."

The C.O.'s took the shackles and handcuffs off us. They made us spread our cheeks and cough and lift our feet and tongue. Then we got in a cold shower.

"That enough. Get y'all out, dry off and give y'all clothes," Fore said.

We put on white boxers, blue jeans pants with *Angola* monogrammed down the legs, and light blue shirt with *Angola* written in white at the back. "Now grab your bed roll and follow me." He pointed out each dorm we were going to. He sent me to Magnolia dorm.

When I walked in, I looked around at all the niggas everywhere. Some were on the phone. Some were laying in their beds, and some were watching TV and playing cards. It was a big open area with a hundred beds lined on both sides in a row. With a big shower area and a small guard booth way in the front.

I walked over to a bunk, and some black ass nigga I don't even know with a scar on his face walked up to me.

"What's up, Slim?"

"My nigga I don't know you. You need to get the fuck out my face."

"What!"

Before he knew it, I punched him in the face. We began fighting. I stepped the nigga, dropping him to the floor. I lost no time in raining blows in the face. I got hands and know how to use them bitches.

"Bitch ass nigga. Do you know me? Don't ever try to play me, bitch. Understand me?" I punched the nigga as I talked to him; blood was coming from everywhere.

Then I saw niggas starting to come around me. Niggas pulling knives. If I'm going to die, I might as well take this nigga with me. Then this black ass nigga stepped in front me with a long ass knife.

"What's up, Stick?" he asked the gang leader with the knife in his hand.

"Man, that my homeboy he fucking up!" Stick replied.

Frowning, I said: "He got what he was looking for. Now we can handle this like some G's or get into some game shit. It don't real matter to me."

"Chill, Slim, it cool."

I looked at the nigga who was talking to me. Sound like he was from the city. I looked from him to the nigga whose face I'd been pummeling. I let the nigga face go. I had blood all over my hands from punching him in the face.

"Now, get you punk ass homeboy up and get the fuck outta here." I watched as his homeboy helped him up.

"What's up, Slim? Where you from?"

"Out the Magnolia."

"Okay, I'm O.G Blaze. I'm out the Melp."

Blaze was built like a linebacker with muscles everywhere and a bald head.

"Where can I wash my hands?"

"Come on, follow me." We walked in the bathroom. It had twenty shower heads in a row with twenty sinks. He watched my back as I washed the blood off my hands.

"You got a homeboy out the Magnolia in here named Mike Mike. You know?"

"Yea, where he at?"

"He's going to be coming out the field in a minute."

"Let's go."

As we was walking out the bathroom, a couple of guys were coming in the dorm. I spotted Mike Mike off the back. He was tall, high yellow, big like the Hulk. And the nigga had good-looking, wavy, black hair with cat eyes. He had two life sentences for killing somebody on a bank robbery.

I was small as a motherfucker running around the project when he used to mess with my mother back in the game.

"What's up, Slim?" He hugged and dapped me off.

"Nothing, coolin'. I just had a fight."

He was looking around the dorm.

Blaze walked up.

"Who he had at fight with?" Mike Mike asked Blaze.

"Bear from Shreveport."

"Oh, that fuck boy. You fuck him up?"

"You know I handle my business."

"Good. Come with me."

We walked over to his bunk. He reached up the bed and handed me a big knife. It had a duct tape and a string on the end. "Go put it up. I'm going to go jump in the shower. I'll holler at you when I get out."

"Good looking out." I walked to my bunk with the knife tuck under my shirt. I stuck it in my pillow. I looked over that the nigga I fucked up. He was holding an ice pack to his face.

Mike walked up to me dressed in black jeans, red shirt, and black all-stars with a red bandanna wrapped around his neck. "What's up, Slim?"

"I'm coolin'."

"You put that thing up?"

"In my pillow."

"Stick it in your mattress."

"Okay."

"You got what you need?"

"I'm straight."

"A'ight, we going to get you right. Your brother told me to look out for you."

"My brother? Where he at?"

"He's on the big yard. Oh, this a letter from him."

I opened it.

***

Slim

One month later, as I walked out the shower area with a towel wrapped around me, I saw somebody walking toward me fast. I had forgot my knife on my bed. As he got close, I noticed it was the nigga I beat up. I pulled the towel off my waist as he charge me with a knife

I moved out the way, punching the nigga in the back of his head. He turned around, swung the knife, cutting me on my arm. I swung a punch, hitting the nigga in his mouth. Then Mike and Blaze ran over, handing me a knife.

We slugged it out. He cut me again on my other arm. I cut him above his eyes. "Come on, nigga, let's roll," I said.

He slammed me on the ground. Mike and Blaze jumped in, and knives went to swing. Everybody for New Orleans and Shreveport was going at it.

The C.O.'s ran in the dorm, spraying pepper spray, putting everybody on the ground.

They had a bunch of us handcuffed while we were bleeding as we lay on the ground, waiting to see the nurse. The nurse gave me nine stitches and bandaged my arm up. They took both of us and a couple of our homeboys to Camp J.

They put me and few of my homeboys in Alligator cell block. And put the other nigga and his homeboys in Gar.

They made me change into an orange jump suit. Camp J was full of cells up and downstairs that were painted pink, with small glass windows on them.

They put me in the cell with a guy close to my age.

"What's up?" I said.

"Nothing. Coolin'."

"Bro, I heard you made it up here. I'm going to look out for you. I got your back. Come, let's go take a walk on the yard. I'm going to give you the game on everything up here. And how shit is ran."

As we walked around the big track, I looked around at the big weight plow, the two big basketball courts. They had niggas everywhere talking, lifting weights, playing cards, smoking cigarettes, smoking weed with the radio playing loud.

White boys on one side, and black on the other. Of course you had punks running around with lipstick on, trying to sell ass or with their menu.

"Look, my nigga. This how this shit goes down. Baton Rouge and Shreveport don't fuck with us at all. They call us city slicker. That nigga you got into it with is from Shreveport. He going to come at you again. Be prepared with that knife you got. On top of that, stay away from the gambling and punks and T.V. That's what get a nigga killed in this bitch quicker than anything."

"Okay."

"Store next week but I got stuff that will hold you over. You smoke?"

"Yea." He lit up for me.

I took a puff. "Shit! This motherfucker strong."

"Old penitentiary cigarette—that what they sell up here."

"I appreciate you."

"Much love." He dapped me off.

I put the blanket on the top bunk, climbing in, laying down. "What you in for?"

"Knife fight. And you?"

"Fight with the C.O."

"Where you from?"

"Calliope. And you?"

"Magnolia."

I went to rapping on one of my raps.

"Who rap that? 2Pac?"

"No, that's my shit."

"Hit that again. It sound good."

"You like that, huh?"

"Yea, you need to do something with it. What's your name?"

"Slim. And you're—"

"Man Man."

"What you in Angola for?"

"Murder."

"I'm in for manslaughter."

"What they give you?"

"Ten. And you?"

"Life. Man, you need to do something with that rap shit."

"I hear you."

Three weeks later, I was on the rec yard talking to my brother. He beat somebody up to come see me in the hole.

"What's up, baby boy? You got big," he said, hugging me tight.

"Nigga, your ass big too." My brother was 6'5 and built like Arnold in *Conan the Barbarian*.

"I heard you got into a knife fight on the yard."

"Yea, nigga was on some bullshit."

"I'm glad you took care of your business."

"You already know. I wasn't about to be no nigga bitch."

"Here." He passed me the cigarette he'd been smoking, letting me hit it. "When you going up for parole?"

"Shit, I keep fucking up."

"I heard. Mom's out there stressing her two sons are in jail."

"Yea, I hear it all the time."

"And I heard you rapping out there."

"Yea, something like that. It not putting no money in my pocket."

"Man, you need to take it serious and see where it can take you."

"I know."

"Look, you got luck this time. Don't get life like me. Do something with your life."

"I understand. But that shit not getting me no money."

"I feel you. But Mike is good people, he that same nigga that help raised us."

"He cool. But we're all in prison."

"Rec over!" a C.O. yelled.

"Love you, lil bro," my brother said, hugging me tight. "Take that rap shit serious. I want to hear your song on the radio."

"I got you, keep your head up."

"You too."

I sat back in my cell, thinking about what my brother said about this rap thing. My cell mate had left, so I had time to rap and write raps for the next two weeks.

Chapter 8

Slim

Back on the dorm, niggas was coming up to me, calling me Slim.

"Slim, man, what's up?" Mike Mike dapped me off.

"Coolin'. See bro back there."

"So, what rap name would you like to go by?"

"As always, *Slim*."

"Yea, I always did like that name of yours."

"Come on, Nephew. Let me show you where you going to stay." I came to find out that *Nephew* is what the old O.G.'s call you up here. Because they're like your old ass uncle.

He handed me a knife. "This the cut where the niggas for the city live and hang. So you stay with us.

"What's up with them niggas?"

"Everything cool. We got an understanding."

"Where the nigga I fought with?"

"They swung him to another unit."

"Okay."

"Yea, you gotta make commissary. Come, I'll take you."

I followed him to this white building where people were in line getting their commissary. You suppose to put your list in, but since I just got out the hole, Mike was going to pull a couple of strings for me.

I walked up to the window, ordered three cartons of humps—all the meats, fish, clothes, tennis, and everything else you could get. I had three bags of stuff; Mike had to help me carry all of it back. I made like $150 worth of commissary. I stuffed all of it in my locker. Then I walked over to the phone, and called my mother.

"Hello," she said.

"I'm out the hole."

"Good. You need to say out of trouble."

"Mom, I'm in Angola. I'm never going to let a nigga play me like a hoe."

"I know how it goes up there. You seen your brother?"

"Yea, he came and seen me while I was in the hole."

"Y'all on the same yard?"

"No. He's somewhere else."

"Okay, when is visitation?"

"Saturday and Sunday."

"Okay, put me on the list I'll be up there this weekend."

"You don't have to come."

"Boy, I know how shit goes down up there with the guard killing people."

"Okay."

"Put Kim on there. You know she want to come."

"I'm calling her now."

"Love you."

"Love you too." I hung up and dialed Kim's number.

"Hey, baby, I was worried about you."

"I'm holding it down like a dog supposed to do. Ya feel me?"

"Yea. Feel you. I miss you. When can I come and see you?"

"My mother coming Saturday."

"Put me on the list. I want to come."

"Okay."

I walked to the cut where I slept at, and grabbed Mike's cell phone. Mike been here so long. He got all kind of shit and make all kinds of moves.

"Hello," Len's voice came up the other end of the line.

"I need you to do me a favor."

"Anything."

"I need you go get me some black Reeboks and send them up here. Then I need you to go holla at my dog Tre. He going to give you a quarter of dope. I need you to sneak it in here."

"I got you."

"I'ma call Tre and tell him to drop off to you."

"Okay. Love you."

"Love you too."

"Hey. What up, Slim?" Tre said, answering his phone.

"Man, I need you drop my girl an ounce dope."

"Nigga, I'm playing with a few ounce of coke."

"Okay, pop her off that. I need you to handle that shit like yesterday."

"I got you."

"That's good looking."

"Nigga, when you coming home?"

"Shit! I don't know, just got out the hole on a knife fight."

"You sling that iron up there, huh?"

"From the street to the pen, it don't stop. Real Magnolia rep."

"Nigga, I'll be waiting for you when you touch down."

"I got this, ya feel me?"

"You know I do. Later."

"Later."

Robert Baptiste

Chapter 9

Slim

I walked out on the visitation floor, dressed in pressed down blue jeans, a red shirt that had *Angola* on the back in white writing, and black boots. My golds were shining, and my hair was freshly fade. The visitation room was big with several iron chairs in a room. Vending machine, and three identical TV's. There was a guard booth that watched over the visitation. Mike had a couple C.O.'s on his payroll. Like I told you, money move shit in here. Along with coke, dope, weed and whatever drug you can get in here. Mike had his hand in everything that move.

I walked up to my mother, hugging and kissing her on the jaw.

"Hey, baby," she said, looking me over.

"Hey, mom. I'm alright."

Kim had on some tight blue jeans, blue blouse, and red heels. Her long black hair was freshly permed and hung to her shoulder, and she smelled so good. I pulled her to me, hugging and kissing her. "Damn! You look and smell good," I said, smiling, showing her my golds."

"You don't look so bad yourself. I miss you, you know!"

"I miss you too."

We went and sat at the table. Kim went to the machine and bought a lot of stuff which she brought back to the table for us to eat and drink.

"Boy, where those knife wounds?" My mother asked.

I showed her my arms and side.

"Lord, have mercy! Boy, you need to chill."

"Mom, I got this," I said, eating on some chicken. Kim and I exchanged shoes. She slid me the dope, and I slid it between my nuts. I got a hundred cash from my mother. You have to pay to play. The guard that supervised visitation charged $100 to let you make it back to the unit. I took a couple of pictures with my mother and Kim. I ended the visitation early so I could move this stuff back before everybody came off visitation. "I love y'all."

"We be up here tomorrow," my mother said.

"Okay. Love y'all both." I walked to the back. The white guard acted as if he was patting me down. He made me take off my shoe that had the dope. I gave him the hundred, and he let me back. Normally, he would strip you butt naked and take what you got and send you to the hole. But Mike turned me on to him.

Mike walked up to me as I walked into the dorm. "Everything good?"

"Yea, it all love."

"Off that ounce of coke—In here I can make like three to five. Dope move a little better. But coke work too."

I showed the homeboys love and then I went to make my own moves. Majority of the white boys was buying that coke. Small bags going for twenty-five dollars. I had my girl bring it in every other weekend. It was lovely.

***

Slim

I was laying on my bunk, getting some more tattoos, and smoking on weed load off of heroin, getting a cross in the middle of my forehead representing the murders I done. I already had the *Magnolia* tattooed on my back, and my name—Slim—on my arm and stomach. I want to be like my idol—2Pac.

I had a couple more run in with niggas in here. They were trying to test a nigga gangster. But it's cool. That why I been turned down by the board for fighting and swinging some nigga about my money. Didn't play without there in the world, and I sure wasn't going to play with it in here.

It's cool. It's the half-way point. I been gone four years. They don't let me make parole this time. Fuck! I have three left to go. You know I'm straight penitentiary now.

"Done," the tattooist said.

"Good looking out."

"Anytime, man."

Using a small mirror, I looked at the tattoos, and was loving what I seen.

I walked over to my bunk, firing up a Joe—which was a slang word for cigarette in the Angola. I grabbed my head phones and put them on, listening to 2Pac album: *Me Against The World*. That one of my favorite CD by him.

Just then, a white boy walked over to my bunk. "Slim," you got something?"

"Yea, what you need?"

"Twenty-five dollars' worth."

"Where the money?"

"Here."

I went in my boot, serving him a twenty-five dollar bag. I laid back in, bed listening to 2Pac.

Robert Baptiste

Chapter 10

Slim

Five Years Later

April 1995

I walked in front the parole board. It was two older women, two white men and one black person. I really didn't want to come to this shit. Because I know once they looked at my jacket, I was hit again. I didn't have my hope on getting out. I had been down five years now. I had three and a half left to go. You do 85% on ten years. So I really don't care what the parole board getting ready to do. Plus they were getting ready to ship us out of Angola. Everybody that had twenty-five years or less was about to get ship to another prison. They were making Angola for people who have fifty years to life.

"Mr. Brown, you are back in front of us," the white woman said, looking at me with all the tattoos in my face. Then she put her head back down, looking at my jacket.

"So if we let you go today, do you have a way to get a job?" the black guy asked.

"Yes, my uncle work for a construction company in the city. He been trying to get me on over there."

"Well, Mr. Brown, today is your lucky day. We going to grant you parole," the white man said, looking at me.

I was smiling on the inside. "Thank y'all," I said, walking out, not even shaking their hands. Fuck the white man, white woman, and the Uncle Tom ass nigga.

I walked to the door; all the homeboys came up to me. "What happen?" they said.

"I got it, ya heard me."

"Nigga, that good," they said, dapping me off. "You know I know ya feel me."

"Nigga, go home and take that rap shit serious. Hold it down for the Magnolia and the city. Be like the renowned 2Pac."

"I got you, Mike," I said, dapping him off. Thanks for everything."

"It's all love," Mike said.

I got on my cell phone, calling my mother and my girl. "Mom, I got parole. I'm to come home."

"For real?"

"Yes."

"I can't wait."

"Love you."

"Love you too, son."

I spoke to Kim next.

"Hello," she said.

"I got parole."

"You made it."

"Yea, I'm about to come home."

"Baby, I'm going to be waiting at the bus station. I can't wait to see you."

"Me too. Love you."

"Love you too."

I laid in my bed, anxious, waiting for 12:01 to hit. That's what time they going to call you for.

"Morris Brown. Get your shit ready. You rolling out."

"That's it, nigga," Mike said to me. Keep your head up. I love you, man. Keep in touch."

"I got you, Mike. You be safe. Holla at my brother for me."

"I got you."

I grabbed my pictures, leaving everything else to Mike. I walked to the front of the dorm where the C.O. was waiting for me. I got in a white van with no handcuffs or shackles. I looked back at the prison, as they pulled off, thinking to myself: *I'm free.*

Now I can put this rap shit down for real.

They pulled up to this little gas station. I stepped out with my pictures. "You free now. Be sure you do something with your life or we be waiting for your ass when you get back." The white and black guys pulled off.

"Fuck you bitches." I walked in the gas station. "Man, let me get a pack of humps and a liter."

"Got you. How long you do in the pen?"

"Five years."

"Man, if you made in that motherfucker, you can make anywhere."

"Gotcha." I walked outside, lit me a hump, thinking about how I was going to get some money to make this rap shit come true. I need me a nice lick.

I saw the *Greyhound Bus* pull up. I dropped the hump on the ground, stepped on it and got in the bus. It wasn't packed with people, so I could lay back and get my mind right.

Robert Baptiste

Chapter 11

Slim

When I stepped off the bus at the Greyhound Bus Station across from the Melpomene Projects, the fresh New Orleans smell hit me. It was like no other smell. They had old heads sitting in the bridge, playing chess and checkers, and niggas—whom we call rock heads in the city—even hustling around the Greyhound Station, trying to rake it in. Shit had changed since 1990. It was 1995, and the city was looking different to me.

Just then, a white 5.0 pulled up in front me with tinted window. I was spook. You know in the city beef never die out. I was beefing with them niggas out the St. Thomas before I left.

As the door opened, I took a step back.

Kim jumped out the car, running up to me. She jumped in my arms, wrapping her legs and arms around me. Hugging me tight. I hugged her back, and we tongue-kissed each other. "I miss you so much." Her eyes moistened with tears.

"I miss you. But I'm home now."

"That right. Come, let's go to my apartment."

As we walked into her apartment, we stripped each other naked. She laid on her back with her legs spread wide. I went down on her, eating her pussy out. I sucked on her swollen fat pink pearl, and tongue it as she gripped my head with her legs shaking.

"Yes, don't stop. I—I—I—I'm cuming!"

I rose up, putting her legs on my shoulders, slamming my dick deeper into her as she came some more.

"Fuck! Slim, I love you. I'm cuming again."

"Fuck! This pussy soft." I began to shake. Her pussy was so warm and wet. It made me come less than a couple minutes.

"Yes, daddy, shoot the hot nut all in this pussy."

I never came so hard in my life. I laid on top her, letting my dick stay there for a minute; it felt so good. When I pulled my dick out of her, she rolled over, deep-throating my dick. She went to sucking my balls and sucking on my dick head, bringing it back to life. She climbed on top of me and rode me like a horse.

She got on her tiptoes, placed her hands on my chest, slamming her ass down. "Fuck! This dick is good. Shit, I'm coming."

Her come ran over my dick down to my legs. She was coming like a water pipe. I flipped her over in a doggy style position, grabbing her hair and slamming against her ass, as I fucked the shit out of her pussy.

"Fuck! Slim, you in my stomach!" she cried out.

She put her head in the pillow as I thrust in and out of her soaking wet pussy. "I'm about to nut."

She went to slamming her ass back on me. "Come in my pussy. Come in my pussy."

I gripped her ass cheeks, shooting all my hot nut inside her.

"Yes, baby! That it. Come in this pussy."

I fell on the bed, trying to catch my breath as she did, and she rested her head on my chest.

"I miss and love you, Slim," said Kim, dosing off.

I got up, put on my clothes, grabbed her car keys, smashing out.

***

When I pulled up in the Projects, everybody was outside. Tre, Len and a few more niggas and hoes ran up to me like I was a celebrity

"What's up, nigga? You home," said Tre, dapping me and hugging me tight.

"You know what it is."

"Yea, we can get this paper."

"Ya, feel me."

"You already."

"What's up, baby? I'm glad to see you home." Len tried to kiss me, but I turned my head.

"I don't know where you mouth been."

"Don't play with me."

"I heard something."

"Boy, that nigga done with."

"Shit! You know how niggas is over hoes in the city."

"That boy in jail. He got ten years."

"It cool. We going to rap about it later." We hugged each other.

I went upstairs to see my mother. I knocked on the door; she opened it up with a big smile on her face. And she hugged me tight as I did the same. I looked like a giant over her.

"I'm glad you home, boy."

"Me too."

"Come in and get some of the red beans and fried chicken."

I sat at the table, eating and talking. "So what you going to do now that you out? I hope the street shit is done. I can't lose another child to the jail system."

I just looked at her.

"So what you going to do? You going to get a job."

"A job? No, won't be doing that."

"So, what you going to do? 'Cause next time your ass go to jail, I'm not going to be there for you. I ain't got time to be running back and forth to somebody jail."

"I'm going to take this rap thing more serious."

"This rap thing. Okay, I hope it going to work out for you."

"It will. I'ma get you a house so you can move out the project."

"Anything that's going to keep you out the streets—I support."

"Love you, mom," I said, kissing her on the forehead, walking to the back. I walked in my room; it was clean. I grabbed me a pair of boxers out the drawer, and jumped in the shower.

I stayed in there for a minute, letting the hot water rinse off my body as I thought about me making a couple of moves. I needed to get in touch with this nigga—Bond—to help me get my career off the ground.

I stepped out the shower, walked in my room, grabbed a polo

shirt and pair of Girbauds, and put on a pair of black Reeboks.

I walked outside. Tre was sitting on the porch, hustling and smoking weed. "What's up, my nigga?"

"What up, Slim?"

"Shit, nigga, I need to get pop out and go shopping."

"I got you. Here a G." He gave me a thousand dollars.

"Good looking."

"I got a lick for us too."

"Yea, I need one of them. I need to pay for this studio time."

"Studio time?"

"Yea, I'm about take this shit serious."

"Okay, I know I fuck with you."

Len came walking outside with some high pink shorts on and pink polo shirt, and some pink Reeboks.

"Slim, what's up with you?"

"I'm coolin'. What you want to be up?"

"Shit! You already know."

"I got to push. I'ma fuck with y'all later. I got to go take my car back."

"That how it is, Slim?"

"For now." If this hoe think I'm going to just give her some good dick and fuck with her after she shit on me when I was in jail, that bitch crazy! She going to have to work her fucking way in. I don't want that bitch on. She was fucking with the nigga Whoo out the St. Thomas, knowing I was beefing with them. I don't know if this bitch trying to set me up or what; I got to get me a tool; a gun, that is!

I jumped in my girl's car, smashing out the project.

***

The next day, Kim and I walked around the mall, picking out clothes.

"Baby, you sure you can afford all this stuff?"

"I got enough save. And besides, when your rap career take off, I need to get paid in full."

"I got you."

We stopped at an outlet store and grabbed several pairs of Girbauds and polos—my favorite clothes.

Then we walked in Foot Locker. I grabbed me two pairs of black Reeboks.

"Boy, you like them Reeboks, huh?"

"I sure do, baby."

"So what stage name you gonna use when you hit the rap scene?"

"Slim, of course."

"Not bad."

"Come, I got to go see the parole officer."

We drove to the parole office. I walked inside the office. I approached the desk and signed the paper. "Name," the black slim lady said.

"Morris Brown."

"You know who you came to see?"

"No."

"Okay, just have a seat."

"A'ight."

"Morris Brown," a white man said.

My parole officer was tall, slim with blond hair and blue eyes.

"Yes, that me." We walked to his office. It was small with a black table, black chairs and a couple pictures on it with a laptop. "My name is Jim Beam. I'm your parole officer. You need to get a job, and if you do it dirty I'm going to violate your ass. You need to pay fifty dollars a month. I see you went to jail for murder but it got broke down to manslaughter. Well, I see what kinda person I'm dealing with. You still in the Magnolia?"

I shook my head.

"Can you pass a drug test?"

I nodded.

I'd just snort a bag of dope, so I got my girl to piss for me in a little tube. I walked in the bathroom, slid her piss in the cup and handed it to him.

"Okay, see you next month."

I just walked out on the cracker. I see he was on some bullshit. Fuck that white man. I got back in the car with my girl. "What happened?"

"I'm dealing a white cracker. Fuck him though. I know I'm going to stay in and out until I get off this paper."

"Baby, don't say that."

"You ain't heard what that cracker said."

"What he said?"

"He know what kind of nigga I am. Fuck that white man. Let's roll."

Chapter 12

Slim

This strip club named *She She* was packed with butt naked hoes running around. Tre threw me a coming home party here. Everybody out the Magnolia was in this bitch. Kim didn't come because she know what it was hitting for. A lot of bitches here and there, and I was going to fuck me a couple of them. Kim just told me to wear a condom.

As I was getting a lap dance from this big ass red bone, one of my throwback bitch walked up to me. She was butt naked. "What's up, Slim?"

"What's up, Brandy? I don't know you work in here."

"A bitch got to do what a bitch got to do."

"I feel you." Brandy was my throwback bitch I was fucking back in the day. She was brown-skinned, short, thick with a big round ass, and short red hair. She use to set niggas up for me to rob. "When you came home?"

"A couple days ago."

"Shit, we need to hook up. I ain't have no good dick in a minute."

"I'm trying fuck you and other hoe."

"I can make that happen."

"And I'm looking for a lick."

"I might got something for you."

"Let me get your number."

"I get off in a few minutes."

"That's what's up."

***

A few hours later, I was in her apartment in her bedroom, watching her and the red bone eating each other pussy out. The red bone had given me a lap dance before they swung into going down on each other.

I watched as they took turns sucking on each other's clit, making each other come as I stroked my dick.

I walked over to them, got in the bed in between them, watched as they took turns sucking on my dick and balls.

Brandy got up, put her pussy in my face, as her friend sucked on my dick.

She climbed on top of my dick, riding me while I ate Brandy's pussy. "Fuck! You got a big dick," her friend said.

She got off me, then Brandy climbed on as her friend sucked on her titties. "I'm coming, Slim," Brandy said, shaking after riding my dick for what seemed like an eternity.

Both of them got into a doggy style position, and I fucked both from the back. I never had two fine bitches at once before.

That why I fuck with this bitch Brandy; she down for anything. She never was my main girl because she was a hoe. And I couldn't trust the bitch like that. "Fuck! I'm coming, Slim," her friend said.

I slammed my dick even harder in her pussy as she shook coming.

I flipped her over, put her legs on my shoulder, thrusting in and out of her until I started shaking.

"I'm about to nut."

"Shoot it all in this pussy."

I pulled my dick out, shooting it all over her stomach.

"Fuck!" I said, cumming.

Her friend licked the rest of the come off my dick. I laid there feeling like a true player. I got up the next morning to go take a piss. I looked around: Brandy and her friend was gone.

Damn! I'm tripping falling asleep at this bitch house. Ain't no telling what this bitch got going on.

As I was coming out the bathroom, I heard somebody walk into the house. I looked around for something I could use to protect myself. Damn! I couldn't find nothing.

As I went to putting my clothes on, she walked in with some food. "You hungry? Where you going? We got some unfinished business."

"No, I'm not hungry. I need some dope."

"I got some on the mirror on the dresser."

"You on this now?"

"You graduate to from weed, coke, to dope."

"You want to be part of what I had got going on?"

"I'm not mad. You was my first everything. You know I was preacher daughter but the first chance I got away, I ran in a thug ass nigga who turned a bitch out to the streets. Now I'm a pro hoe. Here, hit this weed while I suck on your dick."

I laid back, hitting the weed as she sucked on my dick. She climbed on me, riding my dick.

"I miss you, Slim," she whispered in my ear as she rode my dick.

"Bitch! I need you to help me get up."

"I swear I got you, baby. Just hold still while I come all over that dick."

Moments later, she screamed:

"Fuck! I'm coming." She was shaking all over, biting her lips.

***

Later on at night, I sat on the porch in the Magnolia, smoking a blunt, waiting on this nigga Tre. He told me he had something for me. I hope he do. I been home a couple weeks and my pocket wasn't straight. Yea, few niggas give me a couple dollars and bless my game with a couple of ounce of coke, but a nigga need to get right so a nigga can move like I want. I'm tired of using my girl and my mother shit. I was trying to pay for this studio time so I can get serious about this music thing. And hope it would at least get my name out there and help a nigga move out the streets. I'ma always be a street nigga, but at least I can get my mother a house and move her out the bricks.

My brother and them O.G niggas in Angola keep playing in my head: *Do something with your life and that music shit. Don't just throw it away. Fuck with that rap shit.*

For real a nigga trying to be like 2Pac and sell a couple

million. Maybe a nigga can get on with a major label. Who knows! That why I need to get this money.

Just then, Tre pulled up in a black Q45 car. All this nigga been doing since I been gone is hitting lick. He throw me something grand but I need my own shit.

"What's up, nigga?" he said, dapping me off.

"Nigga, about time."

"Let's ride." When we got in his car, he threw a .40 Glock in my lap. "You going to need this. And this mask."

"That's what I'm talking about."

"Man, this a money lick. No dope involved."

"Okay, what we talking?"

"Like a hundred and fifty grand."

"That's what I'm talking about."

"Look, this nigga Jay off Amelia in the 12th Ward. He balling out of control. He got a crack spot that be jumping."

"Shit! You know I'm about that, you understand me."

"Let's ride."

We sat in the car down the street from the pink house on the corner, watching rock heads run in and out. "Nigga, you already."

"Let's do this." As the crackhead was going into the house, we rushed the door, pointing our guns at a fat black nigga, pushing him back in the house. They had a light-skinned hoe sitting at the table. Tre pointed his gun at her.

"Nigga, get on the floor," I said, pointing my gun at him.

"You too bitch!" Tre said.

As Tre went over to get the money, I duct-taped both of them up. "Everything is cool," I said.

Tre ran around the house, looking for the drugs. He found a couple ounces of coke. "Let's bounce," he said.

We ran out the house, jumped in the car and pulled off.

***

We sat at Len's kitchen table, counting the money; it came out to a hundred and fifty thousand dollars, and four and a half of coke. "Len, go lite something up," I said, slapping her on the ass

"Boy, stop," she said, walking off, smiling. "Nigga, I'm sure glad you put me on this money lick."

"I told I had you. This all I been doing, hit money licks. That how I been moving. If I come across work, I sell that shit wholesale. I be on a money chase. That why I beefing with them niggas out the 17th. I grabbed this nigga Ten who was balling. I brought him to his house and got him for eighty thousand dollars, and killed him.

"I feel you."

Len walked back, passing me the blunt. I hit it and passed to Tre as I blow the smoke out my nose.

"Nigga, I'm about to dip."

"Me too."

Len looked askance at me. "Damn! Slim, you not fucking with a bitch for real, huh?"

"Look, I'm going to go put this shit up. I'm going to dip through later."

"Nigga, you said that shit before."

"Man, I'm out." Tre dapped me off.

"Look, Len, I told I'm going to fuck with you."

"Nigga, you ain't fuck a bitch since you been home."

"I got you." I walked out the house, going to my mother's house. I'm going to hold out on that bitch and let her know how it feel to be put on hold when a nigga was joshing.

***

The next evening, I took a shower, got dressed, called my girl to come get me. I needed her to use her credit to get me a truck. I wanted this Eddie Bauer Explorer.

I grabbed my strap along with fifteen grand, and blunt. I walked outside, jumped in my girl car, kissing her.

"Hey, baby."

"Hey, Slim. I thought you was acting funny. I ain't heard from you in two days."

Shit! I been trying to get money right."

"You back at it, huh?"

"You know how I do it."

"Slim, I thought you was going to get into this music thing."

"It take money."

"I get it. Now where you want me to take you?" Kim smiled.

"I need you to co-sign for me a truck."

"What you thinking about getting?"

"1995 Eddie Bauer Explorer."

"Okay, I got you."

We pulled up to Tom Benson dealership on Downman and Chef. When we walked on the lot, I walked up to the black Explorer, checking it out. Then this slim brown-skinned woman walked up to us. "Yes, can I help you?" she said.

"Yea, I want to cop this."

"Okay, let me show you the inside."

The truck was fully loaded with everything. Black leather seat, nice surround sound and whatnot. "Okay, we take it."

"It cost seventy thousand dollars."

"We take it, said Kim."

"Okay, let's go to our finance department and check your credit out." We sat in the office as she ran my girl information.

"Okay, Ms. Smith, are you going to put anything down?"

"Yes, eight thousand five hundred dollars."

"Okay, we'll get it washed for you." The woman smiled, shaking my girl hand.

"Thanks," my girl said.

Before I jumped in the truck, I kissed my girl.

"Love you, baby."

"Love you back."

I came through the hood, flossing my shit. Bitches and niggas was on my dick, wondering how a nigga came up so fast.

I pulled up on the park way, hollering at a few niggas. They was on the set hustling dope. I needed to get in that game. The heroin had the city on lock. And the nigga in the city was getting paid. A few of the niggas around here I know was on a josh upstate. "What's up, niggas?" I said, dapping O.G Glen off.

This nigga been running the parkway for years with the coke and dope.

Glen was a short brown-skinned nigga that did twenty years in Angola back in for murder. "Nothing you made back, huh?"

"You already know. What you put a nigga on with at dilly?"

"You not ready for that." Dilly was another word for dope.

"Shit, uncle, I'm trying to get that money."

'You still fuck around with it?"

"Here and there. You know how it goes."

"Okay, get you money right. I'll fuck with you."

"That's what up."

A few more niggas came out the house, hollering at me and dapping me off.

"Later, I'm going to fuck with you niggas. Y'all be cool."

Robert Baptiste

Chapter 13

Slim

I sat in the house of this bitch named Low. Her place was in the Magnolia streets on the other side of the projects. She was cooking and cutting up crack. Low was a slim chocolate bitch with short gold hair and nice round ass. She a young bitch about twenty-five years old, and she smoked them Mo off and on. *Mo* are crack and weed or cigarette. She cook coke up as her side hustle. Her real hustle is tricking with them older sugar daddy, sucking and fucking them out their check. I brought the key over here because this hoe know how to stretch on key and half. I needed to come up. I chopped off quarter and 50 and 25 slabs as I watched her whip the crack up in the Pyrex pot.

"Slim, your ass is going to stay free this time?" she asked, dropping another and half on the table.

"You know how I roll. If a nigga get out line, I'm going to fuck over them. Or if a lick come my way, I got to see about it. You understand me?"

"Nigga, you need to drop another bounce song. You need to stick to the rap shit."

"Why you think I'm hustling? Studio time ain't free."

Just then my cell phone rang. "It was this nigga Bond. I been trying holla at him since I been home."

"Yo, boy, what happen?" I asked.

"Nigga getting ready to get this money?"

"You already know."

"Okay, meet me at the studio in about two hours, we going to run it."

"I'm already there, you understand me."

"Later."

"Later."

I bagged the crack up and popped her off. I jumped in the truck and headed to the other side of the projects. I ran upstairs, dropped the work off by my mother's house. I grabbed my paper of raps I wrote in jail, along with the 9mm. I jumped back in the truck, headed to the studio.

When I walked in there, Bond was in there listening to another artist he was managing.

"What's up, Slim?" asked Bond, dapping me off.

"I'm coolin'. Listen, I gotta go in the other room and rap for a minute."

We sat in another room, talking and smoking some weed. "Look, this the business with me. I'm trying to take this rap shit serious. I know you can get me where I need to go. But I'm not with the fuck shit."

"What you mean by that?"

I hit the blunt and pass to him. "My money."

"Look, I get ten percent of the show money. And if I can get you a deal with a major label, I'll get a percentage to help manage you. That's the deal."

"What you talking for as being my manager all around?"

"Twenty-five percent to be your manager for everything."

"Okay."

"So when do we hit the studio?"

"Bro, you got to pay for studio time. That will let me know how serious you are."

"I'm not tripping."

"And you got to back away from that street shit."

"Nigga, get serious. How you think a nigga going to pay for this shit? It not free and I'm not getting a job. You managing me. Rest assured you going to get a real street nigga. A dyed-in-the-wool Magnolian. By the way, I plan to go by Slim as my stage name".

"Okay. I'm going to meet you here tomorrow."

"Okay, cool."

As I was coming out the room, I saw DJ Mike. It was my first time seeing him once I been home.

"What's up, Slim? When you got out?" he asked, dapping and hugging me.

"A couple weeks ago."

"So what you going to do with this music thing?"

"I'm trying to take this music shit serious and see where it take me."

"Well, I'm starting a label. I can help you."

"Okay, well, I got couple raps I wrote while I was in prison."

"Look, come down the hallway. I'm in there working with one of my rappers out the Magnolia now."

"Who that be like that there?"

"Young Murder."

When I walked in the studio, I saw a young brown- skinned nigga. He was tall, about 5'9 with tattoos in his face, and a low fade. He was clad in black Girbauds, white polo shirt and white Reeboks with a black bandana around his neck. He came out the booth with a smile on his face, dapping me off.

"What's up, Uncle? Man, when you got out?"

"What's up, Nephew? Damn, you got big!"

"Yea, grown."

"You know each other?" asked DJ Mike.

"Yea, he my nephew on my daddy side." I looked at my nephew. "Boy, when I left, you was stealing cars."

"Yea, Uncle, that was the young me. I'm putting in working, holding the Magnolia down."

"As you should. I see you got a couple teardrops and cross in the middle of your forehead."

"Yea, you getting how I live out here. Beefing with a couple niggas."

"I feel that. Keep holding it down."

"That what's up?"

I sat back down, listened to him rap. He was spitting some fire over the beats. DJ Mike looked at my pad, looking over the raps.

"I got something for that!"

"Yea, let me hear it." I bobbed my head to the beat. Then I walked in the booth and dropped the lyrics to the rap called *You Got It*. The beat and the rap came together beautiful.

"You like that?" I said, walking out the booth.

"Man, that shit was tight."

"You feeling that there, huh?"

"You should let me put this on the compilation album."

"I'm cool with it."

"Later, Murder, you hold it down and keep dropping that fire."

"Much love, Uncle."

I pulled up on the parkway. Stepped out the truck, hollering at a few niggas around there, letting them know I was out of prison. And I got quarters if niggas was trying to cop some coke.

I smoked a blunt with Fat Willie. "Man, I got quarters for two hundred and fifty."

"Okay, I'm going to fuck with you."

"Later. I'm out."

***

Slim

As I was cleaning my truck at the car wash downtown on Claiborne, some nigga pulled up in a red Lexus, bumping my song. He stepped up, throwing the dices up to me.

"Slim, man, that *Slippin'* is fire. When the CD is dropping?" he asked.

"I'm working on it."

"Let me know."

"I got you, man." It had been three weeks since I dropped that track. I know my shit was bumping uptown, but I don't know they were feeling a nigga downtown. I jumped in the truck, pulling off. As I hit the interstate, heading back uptown, I heard a lot of people calling in and requesting my shit on the radio. That shit made a nigga smile, showing all my golds. Maybe this rap shit could work for a nigga.

I pulled up in the Calliope by Rose Tavern, getting out, hollering at Eyes to get me a gram of dope. I had already had some weed and coke. The dope had moved from the St. Thomas to the

Calliope. Each project get their turn to have the fire dope in the city.

"What's up, Eyes?" I said, dapping him off.

"Nothing, coolin'."

"I need a gram."

As I walked to the hallway, getting the dope, I heard them niggas bumping my shit in the project.

"Hey, Slim, that bitch go hard. When the CD coming?"

"The CD on the way."

Eyes handed me the dope. I gave him the three hundred, smashing out.

I pulled up in the Magnolia, sitting in my car with the gun on my lap, a mirror full of dope and coke with a blunt lit in the ashtray.

I snorted a couple of line of both, leaning my head back, hitting the blunt. I didn't realize that I had been sitting there for a minute until somebody knocked on the window and spooked me out. I upped my gun, pointing at the window.

"Bitch, don't play with me," Len said.

I opened the door for her. She got in, taking the blunt out my hand, hitting it. "You almost made me shoot you," I said, nodding with slob coming from my mouth.

"Slim, I need you to take me to the store."

"Okay, let's go."

"Know your ass is high, you not about to kill me. Let me drive."

We traded places. As she drove to a couple different stores, I sat in the car, getting loaded, wiping my face with the towel.

The bitch was looking good. With her red hair hanging and them short tight green jeans, and green and white polo. With her nails and toes done. I ain't going to lie, I want to fuck her. I ain't fucked since I been home.

We made it back to the project. I helped her bring the bags upstairs to her apartment.

We sat on the coke, getting loaded. She snorted a little coke and hit the blunt. She leaned over, unzipped my pants and started stroking my dick.

She pulled her shorts and thong off, climbed back on top of me and slide my dick in her. She went to bouncing up and down on me as I laid back enjoying the ride

"Fuck! Nigga, I been wanting some of this dick since you came home."

I grabbed her ass cheeks, slamming her down on me as she shook, coming.

"Fuck! I'm coming back to back, Slim."

We went in the bedroom. She laid on her stomach as I got on top of her, slamming my dick in her from the back as I suck and bit her on the neck.

"Fuck! This pussy good." I flipped her over on her side, thrusting my dick in and out of her as I grabbed her titties, kissing her as she back her ass up on me.

"I'm coming again."

"Cum, bitch," I said, getting ruffing.

I fucked her about an hour straight, sweating and everything.

As I was hitting her from the back, I began to shake, pulling my dick out, shooting nut all over her ass and back.

We laid in her bed, sweaty and coming, trying to catch our breath.

Chapter 14

Slim

Len woke me later on that night with my cell phone in her hand.

"Who the fuck is it?" I asked, still half sleep.

"I don't know, some bitch that been blowing up your phone all day and night, so I decided to answer it."

I looked at the clock; it was 11 p.m. I took the phone from her before she walked out the room. "What's good?"

"Nigga, you got me out here risking my fucking life while you laid up with some bitch in the project!" Brandy barked.

"Chill the fuck out. Now what's up?"

"I'm with the nigga now, we head to his house. I'm going to call you. Got to go. He coming to the call."

Damn! I forgot I asked the bitch Brandy to put me on a lick. I jumped out the bed, threw on my clothes, and grabbed my gun.

"Where you going?"

"I got to go handle some business."

I grabbed some dope and coke. As I walked out the door, I called Tre.

"Hey, what up, nigga?" Tre said.

"Meet me in the projects. I got something for us." I stepped on the porch, speeding-balling; that's when you mix dope and coke together. I was waiting on Tre to come. I jumped in his car as he pulled up.

"Man, what up?" he asked.

"Nigga, I got a lick for us. Right now. One of my hoes putting me on something."

"Shit, let's push."

"Okay, we heading to the eastern part of New Orleans."

"A'ight"

"She about to hit me in a couple minutes."

"Who?"

"Brandy."

"Man, that hoe stay putting you down."

"That's why I keep the hoe on my team."

My phone rang. "This the hoe right now. What's good, girl?"

"We here now. I'm going to keep the door open for you."

"Okay, what the info?"

"Morris Road."

She hung up. We pulled up to the white brick house on Morris Road in the eastern part of New Orleans. Then a red 500 Benz parked in front of the house. We jumped out the car with our straps in our hands and ran up to the front of the house.

I turned the knob slowly and it opened. We crept upstairs where I heard moaning coming from. I kicked the room door open, pushed Brandy to the side and hit the nigga upside the head with gun. I pulled the nigga out the bed. This nigga—Big Mel—was dark and fat with diamonds and gold in his mouth. His brother was sending him work down from Texas.

I put the gun to the nigga head. "Nigga, this a robbery, don't make it a murder. Now where the bricks and money at?"

"Man, I'm going to check the house," Tre said.

"Nigga, you know who you fucking with? I'm Mel. Out the St. Bernard."

"Nigga, fuck who you are," I said, hitting him again upside the head. He leaned over, holding his head. "Now where the dope?"

Mel was selling heroin; he was getting it from Houston. "Nigga, you going to have to kill me first! I ain't giving you shit. Fuck you, bitch ass nigga!"

"Nigga, you just talking. I don't have a problem with killing your ass."

"Nigga, fuck you. Do what you got to do. Bitch ass nigga, you going to be right behind me."

I shot the nigga twice in the head. Brandy turned around and started throwing up everywhere.

Tre ran upstairs. "Damn! Nigga, why you killed the nigga? How in the fuck we suppose to get the dope now?"

"The nigga told me he wasn't going to give up shit. And I better kill his ass. So I shot him in the head twice."

"Damn! Nigga! He got something in here. Let's search the

room."

We went to trashing the room, flipping over stuff. We found two 9mm Glocks, then we reached the closet.

"I got something a brick of dope," I said, pulling the silver brick wrapped in a red tape.

"I got something too. Some money with rubber band around it."

I went to the nigga's nightstand and dresser, checking the drawers, taking all the jewelry and guns. "He ain't going to need it. Better me than the police."

"Let's be out," Tre said.

Brandy was still there stuck, looking at the dead body. I grabbed her by the hand and ran with her out the house. Even though she put me on licks, she never seen me kill nobody, because either me and Tre go on the lick or I'll go by myself. If she do go, the niggas give it up to where I don't have to kill their ass.

When we pulled up to her apartment in the eastern part of New Orleans, she jumped out the car, running inside.

"Man, you think we should kill that hoe?" Tre asked, hitting the blunt."

"Nah, man, she be fine, just never seen me kill a motherfucker nigga before."

"Okay, cool, I'll let you deal with the fucking drama."

"It's all love."

"A'ight. I'll get up with you in the projects."

"Later, nigga, I said, dapping him off, getting out the car.

When I walked in the apartment, Brandy was in the shower. I took my clothes off, getting in there with her. She turned around, crying, holding me. I tried to tongue-kiss her but she resisted me at first. Then she allowed it to happen. I picked her up, slid my dick into her pussy, and she bounced up and down on it, telling me how much she love me, as her body shook from coming back to back.

She held on for dear life as I slammed my dick deeper and harder into her wet pussy.

"I love you, Slim, I swear I do."

I began shaking, shooting all my hot nut into her. "Fuck! I love you."

***

Jews

I rushed from Houston Texas when I got the call that my brother had been shot and killed. They told me it looked like somebody try to rob him. I had moved from New Orleans years ago. But my brother wanted to stay and run things in the city. I tried to talk him into moving, but he insisted on staying there, telling me it's nothing like home.

So I left him with my crew in the St. Bernard, and I was sending him keys of heroin. I was sending him thirty bricks a month. I was glad them nigga miss the safe in the in the wall. It had twenty bricks of heroin in it. The young nigga that was on his crew told me they got him for a brick of heroin and $50,000. I wasn't worried about stuff they took; it was the principle. To think that the motherfucker would try me and on top of that kill my brother! A nigga or hoe is going to pay for this with their motherfucking life.

I walked in the morgue with my crew to identify my baby brother body.

The mortician pulled the cover back off him. I let a few tears drop from my eyes, as I bent over kissing him on the forehead.

"Fix him up nice, money no problem."

"Will do, sir."

"I swear, baby brother, whoever did this going to pay with their life. They are going to be lying next to you. I promise you that."

I walked outside with my crew. "Boss, what you want me to do?" Pair asked.

Pair was my right-hand man. Tall, brown-skinned with a bald head, we go back to first grade. He put a lot of work in for me back in the day. He came up in the Bernard, slinging and banging together.

"Put the word out a hundred thousand dollars for information on who killed my brother."

"Got you."

"I'm about to take a ride in the projects and holla at my brother crew. To see what they know."

"Okay, I'll let you know if I hear something."

"One, nigga."

I pulled up in the St. Bernard housing projects. They were brownish color bricks and long court ways and driveways. A lot of drugs dealing, robbery and killing goes on back here. This where I first killed a nigga and come up back here. In the 7th Ward St.

Bernard downtown one of the might ass wards in the city.

I stepped out my black BMW, walking in the courtway, looking for my brother crew. They were post up on the steps, selling dope and packing AK-47, smoking on blunts. They looked if they seen a ghost when I walked up on them. Most of my brother crew was my crew except for the young niggas in his crew.

"What up?"

"Jews, what you doing around here?" Black asked.

"Come take a ride with me."

Black was short, dark-skinned with waves in his head. He was my brother right-hand man. I know he had to know something about my brother getting killed.

We jumped in my car, pulling off.

"Who killed my brother?"

"Man, I'm on it now. I got fifty thousand dollars in the streets right now."

"Look, I'm going to take shit back over."

"That's what's up."

"Let the rest of them niggas know. The real boss is back."

"Got you."

"So do you know the last motherfucker he was with?"

"Some bitch name Brandy."

"Okay, bring that bitch to me. I want that trifling dick sucker alive."

"Okay."

"And I got a hundred thousand dollars on whoever head pulled the trigger on my brother."

"I got you. I'm on it."

I pulled back up in the projects, dropping him off.

***

I walked in my brother house with a couple of my crew members. I looked around, then I walked upstairs. I went to his room where everything had been ransacked and his blood was all over the bed. I walked to the closet, looked around. Then I called the crew to bring a couple of hammers. They ran upstairs, and came in the room.

"Look, I need y'all to knock this back wall down in the closet."

They did as they were told. "Okay, boss," they said in unison.

I walked in the closet, looked at the twenty bricks of heroin in silver pack and wrapped with red tape. "Start taking them out and bring them to the truck. I got a storage."

"Okay, boss."

I watched as they pulled them brick from the wall, putting them in the truck. I looked around my brother house one more time and bounced.

I pulled up to the storage room in the eastern part of New Orleans, and had them unload the keys.

"All done, boss."

"Good, now let's find out who killed my brother. Plus I need to find out who he was serving so we can sell these bricks. I don't take losses. The show must go on."

"I feel you," Dirty said.

Dirty was my young head bust out of the project. All he did was, kill. I brought my old crew down from Houston with me.

Dirty was tall, brown-skinned with dread in his head and tattoos all over his face. We jumped in our cars, pulling off.

***

Slim

We sat in Len's kitchen, split the money and keys of heroin. The money was $50,000. "Man, I wonder if this shit good," I said.

"Nigga, let's find out," Tre said.

As I was about to put a couple line on the table, he stopped me. "No, nigga, let's bang the dope. I been stop snorting. I use the needle."

"Nigga, I never bang dope before."

"Nigga, you don't know what you missing. This shit is the best feeling in the world."

He pulled out the syringe.

"Man, that shit clean?"

"Yea, nigga, I don't share needle. That how you get AIDS and shit."

He grabbed the dope, and put some on a spoon with some cut, and drop lemon juice on it. Then he put the fire underneath it. I watched as it melted. I had seen this shit before in Angola when the O.G shot dope. He took his belt off, wrapping it on my arm, making a vein come. I watched as he drew the dope in the needle.

"Hold straight. Don't move."

I watched as he shot it in my arm; it instantly hit me, causing me to go into what was feeling like out of space. I closed my eye, leaning back in the chair, feeling good as the dope hit me. This shit felt better than busting a nut.

"Boy, you going to O.D fucking with that needle," Len said, walking in the kitchen, smoking on a blunt, shaking her head.

I came out the duck load as a motherfucker. I was on cloud nine with my dick rock-hard. I got up went in the bathroom, splashing water on my face. I was too loaded.

"Nigga, you good?" Tre asked

"Yea, nigga, I'm just too loaded, and the dope is fire."

After a couple hours of sitting in the house ducking, smoking humps, the dope started to wear off. I had sent Len to the store to get some foil paper and sandwich bags. I was going to sell my half like Tre, but I thought about it. I need the money. So I'm going to bump the dope back here in the projects.

"Here the stuff," he said, as we walked into the apartment from the porch where we'd earlier chillaxed at after smoking and taking dope in the kitchen.

We were back in the kitchen again for a couple hours, cutting and bagging up dope.

I made a couple simple bags for the dope fiends. You can make a better profit off dope than you can with coke. You see your money better. I would been changed over but I love that boy too much. I would have use it all, and make shit. This shit free, so anything I make on this is a profit.

I grabbed a couple ounces of dope and walked outside. I saw a few dope fiends and gave them samples of the dope.

A couple minutes later, the word was out in the project that I had some fire dope.

Chapter 15

Slim

I had the project bumping with the dope. I convinced Tre to sell me his half. I was making money, hands over fist, even though I was still getting loaded myself.

It was a welfare line outside of dope fiends waiting to get high. I went to serving twenty-dollar bags of dope. They were big flooded.

Plus I was selling three bags for fifty. I had the whole city coming in the project to score dope. I had the Circle on fire.

Tre walked over to me high as a motherfucker, dapping me off as I served the fiends. "What up, nigga? I see you getting this money out here."

"You already know."

I ran in Len's house, putting the money up. I grabbed another ounce of dope, coming back outside, and started serving again.

The morning rush is the best rush. You can make like ten grand less than thirty minutes.

Just then, my nephew walked up. He had on some black Girbauds, white wife beater, black polo draped over his shoulder, and black Nikes. His black 9mm was stuck out his pants pocket.

My little nephew be hanging with the little O.G in the project in the Magnolia court on the other side. They be beefing with everybody in the city. All they do is, rob and kill. I guess they get it from us.

"What's up, Uncle."

"Coolin'. What good?"

"I hear you got that fire."

"Yea."

"Give me two bags."

As I was about to serve him, I heard dope fiend Mary call my name. When I looked up, all I saw was a truck hitting the corner with niggas hanging out the side of it with choppers in their hands.

As I took off running, trying to get the hallway, they went to busting. My nephew up his Glock, hitting back at them. I up my strap, hitting back out the hallway. Tre jumped in the hallway, trying to duck the choppers' bullets that was chipping the project's bricks.

I watched as dope fiend Mary got hit in the head and fell to the ground. As the niggas spunned out the projects, we gave chase, busting the back of the truck window out.

I walked back in the circle, seeing Mary laying on the ground with her head busted wide open. Damn! If she hadn't called my name, that could have been me.

"Them niggas off 3 and G almost caught me slipping," my nephew said.

"Nigga, that your beef?" I asked.

"Yea, Uncle, them niggas killed one of my partner around Club Detour a couple nights ago. So I ran down on their partner at the gas on Claiborne and fuck over him and his hoe."

"Come, let's go before the police start coming back here."

We jumped in my truck, smashing out. "My nigga, you got to be careful when you out here beefing," I said, passing him the blunt.

"I know, Uncle."

"You can't trust nobody else, no bitch. Them hoes try to set you up too. You understand me?"

"I feel you," he said, passing the blunt back to me. "You ain't been in the studio?"

"Yea, I just need a couple more raps then my album done."

"Okay."

I pulled up on Magnolia Street. Them young motherfuckers were out there with choppers ready to go spun on the niggas.

"Be easy, Nephew."

"Later, Uncle."

I pulled off, thinking to myself. I could tell the young niggas to chill because I got my own shit going on. Plus their niggas got killed.

I feel their pain.

***

Murder

I walked over to my niggas. I grabbed the AK-47, cocking it back. "What's up? Y'all ready to ride on these niggas?"

"For sure," Pepper said.

Pepper was my nigga out the courtway. He was brown-skinned with dreads and tattoos in his face. "Let's show this niggas what's up," Joe said, with the AK-47 in his hand.

"Let's prove to these niggas that they can't just spin in our projects," I said.

"Let's ride."

We jumped in the stolen truck and smashed out the projects.

We came to the neighborhood where all them niggas and hoes was chilling on their set. We going to show these bitch ass niggas today. We pulled up fast on them, not giving them a chance to pull their guns. We jumped out, hitting with the choppers, and all the hoes and niggas went to running.

I shot one nigga in the head. I watched him fall to the ground with blood everywhere; a couple of bitches got hit too. As we were pulling off, niggas came out the house. I was shooting at the truck.

I hung out the window, hitting back.

We made back to the project safe, dumped the truck around the block, and ran in this dope house we be selling crack out of.

"Man, we did that shit," Pepper said, snorting a bag of dope.

"You already know," I said, hitting a line of dope."

"Mm, I got to be on our shit now," Joe said, rolling up a blunt.

"I'm out, I'm about to go to my girl house."

"Tell Rena I say hey."

"Nigga, don't play with my girl," I said, walking out.

When I got to Rena's place, I knocked on her back door.

"Who is it?" she asked.

"Me."

She opened the door, wearing grey gym shorts, a grey

bandanna on her head, and barefoot. "What you want?" she asked with an attitude.

Rena been my girl since junior high school. I dropped out and started hustling. She was a thick redbone, with long black pretty hair. Her mother was a crackhead. I be serving her from time to time. She know I be fucking her daughter.

"Why you got attitude?"

"I ain't seen you in two fucking days. I told you I need some tennis and school clothes."

"And I told you I got you."

"I can tell. Probably you were on the other side of the project fucking some them bump bitches."

"Girl, stop tripping."

"I'm not falling nowhere. You high too, huh?"

"You know you like this dope."

"You want to be just like your uncle so bad."

"It that bad thing?"

"I guess not if you don't want to live long."

"Damn! Like that."

"Look, school is around the corner, you going to help me or what? Do I got to ask another nigga?"

"Don't play with me. You go fucking, and get you and the nigga killed."

"Whatever. Nigga, I'm not scared of you."

"Here, three hundred."

She smiled, planting a kiss on my lips, and things went raunchy from that point, making us get rid of each other's clothes, and I had her riding my dick all the way as she moaned with: "Thank you, babe."

Laid back in the bed with my dick hard as concrete, she climbed on top in reverse cowgirl position. I grabbed her fat bouncing ass, her pussy juice dripping all over my dick.

"Yea, ride this dick, you know how I like it."

"I got you, babe," she said, making her pussy clench around my dick while fucking me like one possessed, bouncing atop my dick like mad as she dug her nails into my chest, cuming. "Fuck,

Murder! I love you," she said, shaking.

I flipped her over, gripping her huge ass cheeks, fucking her like a nigga possessed, and pulling her hair, as she put her face in the pillow while taking my dick.

I began to shake as I slammed hard into her pussy. "I'm about to nut."

"Shoot it all in me." I held her ass cheeks tighter.

"Fuck! I love you."

"Love you back," I said, nutting all in her pussy.

Robert Baptiste

Chapter 16

Slim

It's been a couple weeks. The project was still on fire. The police were still everywhere sweating motherfuckers, patting niggas down, pulling niggas over, searching their cars. The police were posted up in the driveway, and courtway. Niggas couldn't make a dime. Mary's murder had the project fucked up. I had to work off my page.

I sat in the studio with DJ Mike, just listening to this fire track of mine. "Man, people been asking for another single," he said.

"Yea, I heard that."

As I was bopping my head to the beat, I looked at my pad that I had in prison. I wrote a rap called *Slippin'*. "I got something for this beat." I walked in the booth, splitting the hook over the beat, and the split fit perfect with the track. I split *Slippin'* on the first take.

I walked out the booth. "You like that?"

"Man, that shit is fire."

"Yea, I was really feeling that shit."

"I see."

"Nigga, you need to get real focus on this rap shit. You never know where it might take you."

"Yea, I feel you, but know I got a lot shit going in these streets."

"For sure."

I just sat back smoking on a blunt, listening to some more track.

***

Slim

When I left the studio, I headed to the mall. I walked in Victoria's Secret and grabbed a couple of thongs and bra for my girl. In her favorite color, along with some perfume that she liked. I had them gift-wrap it for me. Then I stopped at a jewelry store, buying her a tennis bracelet along with a diamond necklace. Then I went to the LV store, got her some heels and a dress she been wanting along with the purse. They hit me for three thousand dollars. I pulled up at the flower shop and bought her dozens of long stem white and red roses. I know she didn't get off until 8:00 p.m. So I made it to her apartment in the east. I walked in, going to the bed room. I looked at the clock; it was 7 p.m. I had an hour to get everything together.

I grabbed the candles out of her drawer, and lit them, letting off a peach smell. Then I dropped the rose petals on the bed and all over the floor, going to the bathroom. I ran a hot bubble bath and lit some more candles.

Then I put the jewelry under the pillow and the rest of the bags in the closet. I picked up the phone, calling Houston Restaurant, ordered steaks, shrimps, and potatoes. It was 7:30 p.m. I headed out, went to the store, got some red wine and picked up the order.

I was hoping I made it back before she reached the apartment. When I made it back, I didn't see her car. I ran inside, setting things up. I didn't have time to take a shower. I hit me a line of dope and rolled me up a blunt, hitting it, waiting on her, to surprise her for her birthday. Just then I heard her keys in the door.

I met her at the door, kissing her.

"Hey, I'm glad to see you." She smiled.

I pulled her chair out, and sat her down. Then I went to the stove, grabbing the food to bring it to her table.

"What all this?"

"Your b-day. Happy birthday."

"And here I thought you forgot."

"I love you, why would I forget that?"

'Well, you running the street fucking other hoes."

"Please can we enjoy your b-day?"

"Okay." After we finished eating, I walked her in the room with my hands covering her eyes. "You ready?"

"Yes."

I took them off her.

"Hey, you didn't have to." She walked over to the bed, picking up the dress, purse and heels.

"You like it?"

"Love it. Thanks, baby," she said, walking up to me, tongue-kissing me.

I walked her into the bathroom, where I helped her get out her clothes and helped her in the tub. Then I started washing her body.

"Baby, I love this. I don't know you had this side of you."

"Only for you."

She reached over, pulling me to her, kissing me. "I love you."

"Love you back."

"Come get in with me."

I took off my clothes, getting into the bath. She grabbed the remote and raised the volume of the blasting Luther Vandross. We went to tongue-kissing. She turned around on my hard dick, sliding it in her pussy, tongue-kissing me. "Fuck, I love you, Slim."

"I love you too."

She rode me for a couple of minutes. Then I picked her up, carrying her to the bedroom. I laid her on the bed, going down on her. I sucked on each one of her toes, then I slide my tongue up between her thighs, as she inhaled while I began licking on her pearl tongue. She exhaled, grabbing my head, grinding her pussy in my face as she came back to back.

"Fuck! I love you, Slim."

Then I moved up her stomach, kissing on it. I placed her brown hard nipples in my mouth, sucked on them as she moaned, biting on her lips.

I flipped her over, licking and sucking on her back as I made my way to her ass cheeks, biting on them. I moved down to her feet, sucked on them before I made my way back up to her ass cheeks, spreading them and eating her ass out.

"Fuck! Eat this ass."

After I rimmed her asshole out, I flipped her over and we 69 each other; as she suck my dick, I ate her pussy out. Then I put her legs on my shoulders, slamming my dick into her walls as she tongue-kissed me, telling me how much she love me.

She got on top, rode my dick as I gripped her ass cheeks, bouncing her up and down on my dick as she came like rain. I flipped her on her side, slamming my dick in her from the side as I suck and bit on her neck, with her ass cheeks in the air.

"I'm about to nut," I said, shaking.

She pushed back on me as she held my ass tight. I couldn't move as she gripped my neck.

"Yes, come in me."

I shot hot nut all in her as she came all over my dick. We lay there for a minute, catching our breath. She laid her head on my chest as I played in her hair.

"Thank you for the gifts and the roses and a beauty b-day."

I reached under the pillow, pulling out the jewelry box. "Here."

"What this?" She rose up.

She smiled, opening both of the boxes. "Damn! Baby, thank you. I love it so much."

"What? You thought it was a ring?"

"Yes, but I'll take this."

"A ring coming."

"Better," she said, pulling the jewelry on. She climbed up on me, sliding my dick into her still soaking wet pussy.

"I love you so much," she said, kissing me.

"Love you back. I reached out my hands and brought her face to mine, kissing her.

We made love all night.

***

Tre

I rode around the city, looking for this nigga Ray. This nigga Kevin paid me ten grand to kill this nigga. I need them ten grand to get dope, coke and weed and buy my girl shit. A nigga been fuck up. I need another lick for real. Just then, my phone rang.

"Hey, what, nigga?"

"You coming to the club, nigga? You know nigga about to throw down."

"Nah, I got to handle some business. But hold down for the project."

"You already know. Later."

"Later." I pulled over, pulling my needle out that was mix with coke and dope. I shot in my arm. Then I pulled off. with a murderous look on my face and the chopper on the seat.

As I pulled up to this nigga house, I spotted his Lexus cop in front his house. To my surprise, this nigga was talking to some red bitch. I parked down the street. Then I grabbed the chopper off the seat and creep down on the nigga with my chopper. He never saw me coming.

I rose up, loading on the whole car, shooting at least thirty rounds, killing everything inside. I ran back to my car, pulling off.

I picked up my phone, calling this nigga Kevin.

"What's up?"

"Nigga, it done."

"Look, come through, I got a key for you."

"Good looking."

"Later."

***

Slim

I walked in this club with my gun in my waist. The club was called *The Corner Pocket*. It was down the street from Magnolia. One of the big time drug lords out the Magnolia own it.

He paid me a few stacks to come perform my song: *You Got It*.

It had the city on fire. My single had the compilation CD selling out Peaches record store. It move 10,000 unit. My song was blowing up on the radio station. People was calling in requesting my shit. I was the hottest rapper in the city.

I had the Magnolia on the fucking map. You already know I rep the Magnolia to the bone. I had my song poppin' on the outskirt too. Kenner, Slidell, Metairie and couple more surround areas.

I jumped on stage with some black Girbauds, red polo shirt, black Reeboks, and the mic. It was about five hundred people in there.

When the beat dropped, the crowd went crazy, rapping the song with me. *"If you got it, I want it, let me get it out here, so drop it, ain't not stop it—"*

They sang every word with me.

When I stepped off the stage, niggas gave me dap, and hoes gave me hugs.

As I was chilling at the bar sipping on a drink, I saw Tre walking toward me. He'd told me he had some business to handle.

"What's up, nigga?" I asked.

"Coming to fuck with you."

"I thought you had some business to handle."

"Yea, I got them ten G bust a nigga up out the ward."

'What!"

"Yea, nigga had ten on the nigga head for some shit he did."

"Who?"

"Come, let's dip."

We left the club and made it to the project and sat on the porch, shooting dope and talking.

"The nigga Ray. He jacked some nigga out 13th for four bricks of coke."

"Who he jacked? Kevin?"

"Yea, I want to get this nigga Kevin. I heard he got that work. He gave the nigga four and then ran off so I took the hit. Fuck him and the hoe he was with. Caught him slipping in front his house sitting in the car talking, then ran down on them, shooting them up all in the body and face with the chopper.

"I feel you."

"Nigga, the album on fire."

"It cool. But a nigga getting few dollars, yet you know nigga still got to get it out the streets."

"I feel you."

"Slim, you got some crack?"

"Yea, what you trying to get?"

"Forty."

"Okay, I pulled the crack out my pocket, exchanged it for the money."

"Thanks."

Next thing I know me and Tre was nodding out and the sun was coming up. Len walked outside, calling our name.

"Slim, Tre, what the fuck y'all doing?

We raised our head up with slob coming from our mouth, looking at her with our eyes barely open.

"Huh?" we said,

"Man, nigga going to fuck you niggas up. Y'all slipping." We went back in the duck.

Robert Baptiste

Chapter 17

Slim

As I stood at the gas station on Claiborne, getting gas loaded with a big black .40 on me, a black on black Lexus car pulled up on me. I ain't going to lie: a nigga was spooking for real because a nigga beef with a lot of niggas in the city. I clutched my gun just then. My bitch Tracy stepped out, looking good. She had on some tight pink shorts on riding in her pussy and had her cheeks hanging out. With a pink halter top that was holding her big titties in place, her hard nipples pointing out. Her hair was cut short and dyed red.

The hoe use to send a nigga some money and naked pictures.

"What's up, Slim? You ain't holla at a bitch since you been home," she said, walking up on a nigga.

"I ain't had your number, you know you be changing your number."

"Well, you know a bitch be moving."

"I see you doing good."

"Something like that." She hugged and kissed me on the lips.

"I see you ass got finer."

"Yea, but a bitch ain't had no good dick in a minute."

"Shit, I know you lying."

"I tell you these niggas ain't shit out here. All the real niggas in jail."

"I hear you."

"Well, what you about to do?"

"Head back in the project and get some money."

"Won't you go to a hotel with a bitch? I'm trying to get fuck."

"Look, give your number."

"Look, nigga, here you go," she said after putting her number in my phone. "I'll be expecting you at the hotel. I'ma text you the name and address soon."

"See you there once I'm done handling my business in the project."

"Later."

"Sure."

When I walked into the hotel room, she was naked like she came in the world. She undid my pants and dropped to her knees, stroking my dick. She went to deep-throating it like a porn star. The bitch was a pro; she didn't even gag on it. She pulled it out, spitting on it, and put it back in her mouth. She sucked on the head until my body started to tense up. My eyes rolled in the back of my head, my ass cheeks got tight. Then she sucked on my balls until I started shaking.

"Fuck! I'm about to bust."

She put it back in her mouth, sucking real hard until I came all in her mouth.

She swallowed all my nut like it was water. Then she sucked my dick until it got back hard. She got in the bed, spreading her legs as I slammed my dick into her soaking wet pussy. I put her legs all the way to the head board and had her ass up in the air as I slammed down on her pussy. She couldn't run; all she could do was, scream and take this thick black dick.

"Fuck! Slim, please, baby, I'm sorry."

I wasn't trying to hear shit. I was beating her pussy up as she screamed my name while she shook and came. Then I flipped her over, thrusting my dick into her pussy, holding her waist as she tried to run. "Fuck! Slim, you in my stomach."

"Shut up, bitch, take this dick, you ask for it."

"I—I—I—I'm cuming!" she stuttered out as she shook.

I shook as I slammed deeper into her.

"I'm about to cum," I said.

She slammed back on me hard as I slammed against her. She rammed her ass back on me as I shook and shot my nut all in her pussy.

***

"Damn, boy I'm glad you home. A bitch ain't have no dick like that in a minute," Tracy said, as she watched me put on my clothes. "Fuck! I miss that dick. You got to put a bitch on a payroll or something."

"I got you. Call me later."

I grabbed my gun, walked out and jumped in my truck, pulling off.

I sat with my gun on my lap, smoking on a blunt. Next thing I know, a car rolled up on my passenger side with the window rolled down, and bullets went to hitting my truck door, and the window shattered. I hit the gas. As I sped away, I started getting weak and passed out.

When I came through, I was sitting in a hospital bed. I tried to move but it hurt me on my side and arm. I looked up, and Tracy was there. I had several bandages on my waist and arm.

"Damn! Slim, nigga, you scared the shit out of me," she said.

"What happen?" I asked.

"Nigga, I was right behind you, and a blue Chevy rolled up on you busting and pulled off.

Just then, the doctor came in the room. "Mr. Morris, you're lucky. How do you feel?"

"A lil' sore."

"Okay, the bullets went in and out."

"When can I leave?"

"We would like to keep you overnight."

"Well, doc, I'm good. I don't need no niggas killing me in the hospital."

"Okay, I'm going to get you a prescription for some pain pills."

"Okay, doc," I said, getting up, hurting as Tracy help me put on my clothes.

"You sure about this?" Tracy asked.

"Yea, never been sure in my life. Take me home."

"Okay."

"No, on second thought, call Tre to come get me."

"Why? You going by Kim?"

"Don't start."

"Okay, I'm going to let you make it because your ass shot."

I got in Tre's car, and he pulled off. "Nigga, you good?"

"I'm hurt like shit."

"You know who did this?"

"No, I wish I did. Their ass be fuck up tonight."

"Nigga, ain't no telling you beefing with so many niggas in the city. I told you that nigga Wayne got money on your head."

"I know. I just need time to figure this shit out. Drop me of by Kim."

"Okay." When I walked into Kim's apartment, she came out from the kitchen, staring at me with a blank look on her face. "Babe, what happen to you? Where that blood from?"

"I got shot today."

"What! Where!" she said, walking over to me, feeling me and raised my shirt up. "Are you alright?"

Next thing I know, I collapsed in her arms. The next evening, I woke up in so much fucking pain. I got up sore as a motherfucker, walking over to the drawer, grabbing the pain killers. I popped the pain killers and grabbed a bag of dope, making me a line. As I was about snort it, Kim walked in the room.

"Boy, what are you doing?"

"Killing this pain," I said, snorting a line.

"Come get in the bed so I can change the bandages. I called the hospital. They told me it was nothing they can do because bullets went in and out. Just change the bandage. Which I already know because I'm a nurse. Look, you need to slow down."

"Please don't preach to me. Not right now."

"Somebody need to talk sense into you."

"I'm good right now."

"I can tell you're not."

"It's all good." I didn't feel like hearing this shit. That's why I haven't move in here with her yet. I can't go through all this shit with her all the time. I'm good.

"You need to stay home for a couple weeks and heal."

"Okay," I said.

"I'm serious."

"Okay."

"I'm going to work. Love you."

"Love you."

Robert Baptiste

Chapter 18

Jews

I sat at the bar across the street from the project, watching the sports, waiting for this nigga Steve to come and holla at me. He was supposed to be taking that motherfucker out for a hundred thousand dollars. He was a young nigga out the project trying to get some heads belt. I heard he was supposed to have shot the nigga or something.

He walked in the bar, walking over to me. My nigga Black patted him and took the 9mm off him.

"Let him come in. What you got?"

"I shot the nigga, but he live."

"I thought you say you was the man for the job."

"I am."

"So why the hoe and nigga still living?"

"Man, I unload the clip into the nigga car," Steve said.

"Well, I need the nigga dead. You need to make it happen."

"I got it."

"I thought you know who the bitch was with my brother."

"I'm on it."

"I need you to bring that bitch to me."

"I got it."

"Don't come back with something or you ass going to be in a box and the consequence going to be on your head.

I watched as Black gave Steve his pistol back, and he walked out.

***

Len

I sat in the hair salon of my friend—Porsche—in the eastern part of New Orleans, about to get my hair done.

Then I heard a couple bitches mentioning Slim and Tre names.

I faked like I was reading a magazine, listening to these dump hoes talk. I see why Slim and Tre jack so many in niggas in the city.

Because a lot of these niggas that got money pillow talk with these freak bitches and tell them all their business. And when Slim or Tre fuck them dump hoes, they put Slim and Tre on them dump ass niggas.

As I listen to them, they talked about this nigga Jews out the St. Bernard.

These hoes were strippers. One was high yellow with long red weave in her head, and the other one was a red bone with long blue weave. Both them hoes were tore up.

"Bitch, you know Jews back in town."

"I heard," the high yellow said.

"Yea, use to fuck the nigga back in the day."

"Bitch, for real?"

"Yea, we go back to junior high."

"But I heard the nigga back in town because a nigga killed his brother."

"Yea, I heard it was suppose to be Slim and Tre out the Nolia. All they do is jack big time dope boys."

"Well, I heard Jews going to put that money on their head."

"Word on the street says he got a hundred thousand dollars on their head."

"Bitch, I wish I was a killer," the red one said.

"For sure," the yellow said.

Without waiting for them hoes to finish the conversation, I slid off the salon, calling Slim.

***

Slim

Two weeks later, I was riding around the city in my truck with a .40 Glock on my lap, trying to see if I heard something in the streets about who shot me up.

I need to find out the nigga that was trying to get rid of me. I know the nigga Wayne out the 10th Ward had ten grand on my head. I been trying to find out where the nigga stay because I was going to smoke his ass.

As I blew the smoke out my nose, my cell phone rang.

"What's up, Len?"

"Where you at?"

"Around."

"I need you to come holla at me."

"About what?"

"Nigga, this important?"

"Where you at?"

"At Porsche Salon in the East."

"I'm on my way."

As I drove to the eastern part of New Orleans, I hoped this bitch wasn't on no bullshit. I hoped Len had some shit for me on who shot me up.

When I rolled down the street, I spotted her standing on the corner.

I pulled up on her and she got in. "Why you staying on the corner?"

"Because I don't want them hoes to see me get in the truck with you."

"Man, fuck them hoes."

"Nigga, not like that. They was talking about some nigga out the seven ward named Jews. The nigga got a hit on you for killing his brother."

"Damn! Love, thanks. What else did them hoes say?"

"That the nigga got a hundred grand on you and Tre head."

"That's good looking out."

"Nigga, I need two hundred dollars to get my hair fix."

I dug in my pocket, giving her the money.

"Thanks," she said, kissing me. "Drop me back on the corner, Slim."

I pulled up on the corner, letting her out.

"Nigga, I need some dick too."

"I'm going to spin in the project later on."

"Bye."

I pulled off, dialing Tre's number.

"What the business is?"

"We need to talk."

"Okay, I'll meet you in the bricks."

"Later."

***

Slim

I pulled up in the Iberville projects in the 4th Ward down town where this nigga Tre's girl lives. He came running out the hallway with his gun in his hand, getting into my car as I pulled off.

"What's up nigga? You better be on some life and death situation. I was getting me some pussy."

"Nigga, you know it is."

"Lay it on me."

"Len told me that some nigga name Jews out the seven ward got a hit on us for killing his brother."

"Damn! What they talking."

"A hundred thousand."

"Okay, you know where this nigga hanging?"

"No, but I'm going to get my bitch Bam to find out."

"Okay, hand that shit."

"Where you want me to bring you?"

"Back by my girl." I pulled up in the projects, dapping him off. "Later."

"Later, my nigga." I pulled off, called this bitch Bam out the St. Bernard.

"Hello?" she said.

"I'm about to come through."

"Okay."

Later that night, I crept through the Bernard, picking her up. "Slim, when you got out?"

"Nine months ago."

"And you just now calling a bitch."

"I been busy. What you know about a nigga put a hit on me?"

"What it in for me?" She smiled.

"What you want?"

"You already know.

I pulled up in the Magnolia and took her by my mother's house.

When we hit the room, she fell back on the bed butt naked. Bam was a thick chocolate bitch I use to fuck with when I was going to junior high school. She from out the Magnolia but move in the St. Bernard.

She a good girl but got a thing for street niggas. I broke her virginity with that dope dick and been fucking her ever since. I don't care who she fucking with; when I call, she come running.

I put her legs on my shoulder, thrusting in and out her pussy as she dig her nails into my back, screaming my name.

"Fuck me, Slim, fuck me. Please don't stop, I'm coming."

She started shaking, coming all over my dick. I flipped her over, pulling her to the end of the bed, slamming my dick into her. I stuck my finger in her wet asshole. "Fuck! This pussy fire."

"Yes, daddy, fuck this pussy."

Her pussy stay nice and tight. I'm not going to lie to you: I love this bitch, but we can't be together because every time I got to jail this bitch leave.

She just not the jail type. But the hoes give me pussy every time I come home. "Fuck! I'm about to nut."

I pulled my dick out, shooting come all over her ass and back. She got up and went into the bathroom as I laid back in the bed, lighting up a hump, smoking it. She walked back in, getting into the bed, and fired the blunt up.

"Now tell about this nigga."

"You killed this nigga Jews brother. Jews is a big time dealer who came back from Houston to find out who fucking his brother. He running things now with heroin in our project."

"Who took the hit?"

"Some young nigga name Steve."

"Okay, thank you."

"That what up. You know a bitch still in love with you. I just can't do that jail shit." She blew smoke out her nose.

"I feel you, that why I got me a main bitch."

"Cool, as long you give me the dick when I want it. I ain't tripping."

"You know what that nigga look like?"

"Yea."

"Where he be hanging around the project?"

"You going to have to show this nigga."

"I got you."

She rolled over, climbed on top of me and began riding my dick.

"I fucking love you."

Chapter 19

Tre

I sat on the porch in the Magnolia in the dark courtway with my gun on my lap, serving coke bags.

I went on a hustle by myself, jacked a nigga out of a couple keys of coke and $25,000. One of my hoes put me on a lick.

As I was hitting the blunt, this bitch Kelly out the project that I fuck from time to time walked up on me.

She was slim, black as midnight with short blue hair. She had on some tight pink shorts that were all in her ass, and pink wife beater together with white house slippers. She was fine, and a hood bitch.

She was supposed to have a baby for me. But she be fucking every dope nigga in the city. I don't know if the baby was mine or not.

Because every time I tell the bitch to let's go take a blood test, the hoe never show up.

I'm not going to lie: the bitch got some good head and pussy. And I give the hoe money from time to time to take care of her two boys.

"What's up, Tre?"

"Nothing, coolin'. What's good?"

"You think you can run me to the store?"

"Walk your ass around the corner."

"Boy, I need to go to the store by the Melp."

"Man, you just want to be seen with a nigga."

"Boy, whatever, and I need a few dollars."

"Man, you need too fucking much. Where them niggas you fucking?"

"Boy, fuck them niggas. You going to help me or not?"

"I got you. I dig in my pocket, giving her a hundred dollars.

I pulled up to the 24-hour store around the Melp. I know my black ass shouldn't be over here.

***

Dirty

As I was riding uptown looking for these niggas, I spotted this nigga Tre going into the store by the Melpomene Projects. He was walking in there with some bitch.

"That's that nigga right there, Bee," I said.

"I see him." Bee was one the young niggas out the project that was about busting head.

I pulled over, parked my car a couple blocks down. "We going to wait for this motherfucker to come out."

"For sure."

"We going to run down on this nigga and kill him and that bitch."

"I'm with that."

"We going to get them hundred thousand grand."

"Yea, I need that money. I can get me a whip with that."

"That's what's up."

"There that nigga goes right there."

"Let do this."

We stepped out the car with our guns in hand.

***

Tre

As we were coming out the store, I was holding the bag, fussing with this dumb bitch, telling her she need to get her life straight.

Then all of a sudden she screamed out my name.

"Tre, look out!"

I turned around to see two niggas running my way, holding guns.

I pulled my gun and went to hitting.

Boom! Boom! Boom!

I ducked behind the truck, pulling Kelly down to the ground, as they bust back.

One nigga gun jam. I jumped up, hitting the nigga in the chest.

The other broke out running as I shot at him. I shot a few people car windows out, trying to get at him.

He jumped in the truck, smashing out.

I grabbed Kelly off the ground, shoved her in the car and smashed out.

We walked in her apartment. I sat on the couch as she walked from the back, lighting up a blunt, and sat next to me on the couch.

"Boy, them niggas almost had your ass," she said, passing the blunt to me.

"Yea, fussing with your trifling ass," I said, hitting the weed before passing it back to her.

"Nigga, don't blame me for your beef shit. If it wasn't for me screaming, them nigga would have had your ass."

"That real. I'm glad you had my back and didn't freeze up."

"I told you I got you." She got up, pulled her shorts off. She unzipped my pants, getting on top of me, inserting my dick in her wet pussy and began riding me. "I got you."

Chapter 20

Slim

I was standing in the studio, listening to this new track Mike had sent me. "Man, this beat is slamming."

"It is, huh?" the engineer said.

Just then, Bond walked in the studio with a big smile on his face. "Man, what's good?" I asked.

"Man, I got some good news."

"Nigga, what it is?"

"The label Hype Records want to sign you."

"For real?"

"Yea. They got a little deal with Tomboy Records. They heard your single."

"Okay, we can go see what they talking about?"

"Plus they talking about giving twenty-five thousand dollars on signing bonus."

"Okay, I can fuck with that."

"Man, this just a start to get your name out there. That why I been tell you. You can't have one foot in and one foot out. This rap shit can blow for you."

"Man, the streets is my life; that where I'm from. I'm going to be in them until I'm dead. Thugging and drugging—that me."

"I get that but you got to find a way out."

"I got you."

Just then, my phone rang. "What's good, nigga?"

"Man, some nigga try to kill my ass last night!"

"What! Where you at?"

"In the Nolia."

"Okay, I'm going to come in a couple minutes."

"Later."

When I pulled up in the projects, Tre was sitting on the porch steps, smoking a blunt. "What's up, nigga?" I said, dapping him off.

"Man, this motherfucker try to kill me last night."

"Who?"

"I think it was them nigga from downtown."

"What happen where you was?"

"I was at the store around Melpomene."

"Man, I told you about being around there. You know we beefing with them nigga. You sure it was them and not them nigga out here project?"

"Yea."

"What happen?"

"Man, it was a corner out the store around there when two niggas try to creep on me. Good thing Kelly seen them or my ass was dead. I up my gun and went to shooting. I killed one nigga but the other nigga got away."

"Damn, nigga, I'm glad you made it."

"Nigga, me too. I'm trying to ride on these niggas tonight."

"Nigga, it going to have to wait. I'm going out of town. Hype Records want to sign me. I'm finally going to get look at."

"Nigga, that cool, but while you in recording, I'm here dealing with this beef shit."

"Damn! My nigga, that how you feeling? I'll never leave you hanging."

"Nah, I'm happy for you, my nigga," he said, dapping me off.

"We going to handle business."

"Well, good luck with that."

"Nigga, you tripping on that bullshit with them niggas."

"Man, while you're in the studio, I'm the one getting shot at."

'Damn! Tre nigga. I got your fucking back, nigga. I'm in the war with you. I'm not going to leave you hanging."

"I hear you," he said, blowing the smoke out his nose.

"I'm going to holla at my girl. Later."

"Later."

***

Slim

When I walked inside, Kim was cooking. I walked in the kitchen behind her, kissing her on the neck and rubbing on her ass. "Hey, baby. You in a good mood."

"Yea, I'm. Well, because a record label want to sign me."

"For real?"

"Yea, love."

She hugged and kissed me. "I know you was going to make it."

"They can help me get my name out there. They got deal with Tomboy Records."

"Okay, I love it. It's a start for you."

"Thanks, baby."

"So that mean we can move in together."

"I don't know about all that."

"What about have a kid?"

"We can work on a baby."

"Okay, I love you."

"Love you back."

"So you giving up the street life, right?"

"I don't say all that." I pulled her to me, tongue-kissed her, pulling her pants down, bending her over the couch. I thrust my dick in and out of her wet pussy as she backed up on me, as I pulled her hair and slapped her on the ass.

"I'm coming. Baby, don't stop!"

We laid on the floor in the living room with her laid on my shoulders while I thrust in and out of her, as she dug her nails into my back, telling me how much she love me in between her coming over and over.

I was shaking as I shot all my hot nut into her warm wet pussy.

"Yea, give it all to me!" she moaned.

We laid on the floor, trying to catch our breath.

Robert Baptiste

Chapter 21

Slim

The next day, Bond and I went across the river to Hype Records. We sat in there with a black guy named Larry Wilson. He was tall, about 6'0 feet with waves in his hair, and slim. He had an all-gray suit on.

"What's good, Slim?"

"Nothing, coolin'. Trying to see what you talking about."

"Well, I heard your single. And I would like to sign you for album deal."

"What you talking?"

"We give you one video. Twenty-five thousand dollars up front."

"What else?"

"Well, I just sign a deal with Tomboy Records. If shit goes right, I sign you to another deal."

"Okay, what we talking I get off an album?"

"Well, I give you fifty percent. That's after I make my twenty-five thousand back."

"You can keep that. I'm going to make money in the streets."

"Well, I don't want you doing that."

"Nigga, you must don't know who I am. I was Magnolia Slim first. I get money out the streets."

"Okay, well, I just want you to stay out the streets so we can get this money. And get your name out there."

"I hear you."

"Look, take the twenty-five thousand grand. It will hold you over until the album come out."

"Okay, where the contract? Let Bond read. I got somewhere to be."

"Okay."

I signed the contract for the one album.

***

Slim

I sat in the studio a couple of months later, laying down the last song.

Mike gave me some new fresh beats. Bond was talking about the need to make the video. They got this new video channel called Phat Phat and all that we need to get my video on.

I walked in the booth, laying this rap called *The Dark Side Down*. "What you think?" I asked.

"I like it. We need two more. Then we finish."

"That's what's up." I sat back down, rolling up a blunt, singing to the tracks, trying to come up with some raps.

Bond walked in the studio.

"Nigga P trying to get you on down South Hustlers."

"You serious?"

"Yea, nigga, this could be major for you."

"For sure. What he want?"

"A song."

"Okay, I got one for him."

"Which one?"

"Bouncing and Swinging."

"I thought you was going to put that on your own album."

"Nigga, this major."

"Okay, give it to him," Mike said.

"Alright."

"Nigga P. For real," I said, hitting the blunt.

A few weeks later, we were staying in the middle of the Magnolia, getting ready to shoot my video for *The Dark Side*. That's the name of my album and the song we about to shoot for. The label gave me $100,000 budget.

I had the hold on Magnolia Project outside. I was waiting on this nigga Tre to show up.

When he showed up, he had on some blue Girbaud shorts, white polo shirt, and blue polo boots.

I had on some black Girbaud shorts, black wife beater, a Black

Saints jersey draped over my shoulder with the black Reeboks. I had a penitentiary hump in my mouth with a black bandanna wrapped around my neck.

"Y'all ready?" I asked the project.

"Y'all let's go," they said.

As camera went to rolling, I went to rap my song *The Dark Side*, and the whole hood show out. Everybody jumped in the video, repping the Magnolia.

The shit was dope. Hoes was shaking their ass, twerking all for the cameras. Nigga was getting their stunt on.

I was loving it, showing love to my hood.

"That's a wrap," the director said.

"Nigga, that shit was live," Tre said, dapping me.

"For sure."

"Nigga, what you getting it?"

"Shit coolin'. Why?"

"Shit, we can go hit some hoes up."

"I'm with that."

As they were wrapping all the stuff up, niggas spun the corner, hanging out a black truck, shooting at me and Tre. People ran and screamed, ducking and trying to hide. I ran in the hallway, grabbed the chopper, busting back out the hallway as Tre shot back with his 9mm, ducking in the hallway.

"Damn! I wonder who hit the project like that!" I said to myself.

I stepped out the hallway, looking around with the chopper in my hand, making sure they were gone and not spun back.

"Damn! Them nigga blow my fucking high."

"Damn! I need to find out who that was. And deal with their ass."

"For sure."

"Man, we can't even do a video without getting shot at," Bond said.

"This my life."

"You got make a choice. You can't have one foot in and one foot out. It don't work like that."

"I'm street first then rap."

"I hear you."

"Let's go find out who that was," I said to Tre. We jumped in the truck and pulled off.

Chapter 22

Slim

My nephew and his crew and I sat on the porch in the project, smoking and talking, waiting on Wild Wayne to show up. A couple minutes later, he pulled up in his white truck.

Wild Wayne was brown-skinned, tall with curly hair.

He walked up in the porch with his mic out.

"What's up, Slim?"

"Shit coolin'."

"For sure. I see you real be in the Nolia."

"Yea, you know I rep this shit all day. We ain't playing back here. All the BG's show their guns."

I grabbed the chopper out the hallway, showing it off. "It ain't no game in real life."

"Okay, then. What the name of the album going to be?"

"The Dark Side."

"I heard P reach out."

"Yea, put me on down South Hustlers."

"Yea, you dig he show love to a real nigga. So what you think the album going to do?"

"I hope it sell hundred thousand."

"It might go gold, it fire."

"I hope."

"So who you sign with?"

"Hype Records."

"Okay. Well, we going to show your video."

"A'ight. Thanks for the love.

"For sure."

***

Slim

I was knocked out, sleeping with Kim on my chest when I

came back. I moved in with her, but I kept my mother's house in the project in case this shit don't work out. Because once you move in with these females, shit change and they be trying to be on some control shit.

My phone rang. "Hello."

"Nigga, you still trying to do this video or what? We waiting on you."

"Damn! My nigga, I'm on the way." I got up.

"Babe, where you going?" Kim rolled over, half sleep.

"I got to go do this video."

"I want to come."

We jumped in the shower together, getting a quickie.

We hurried up and got dressed.

Everybody was outside waiting on me. The whole project was out there again.

"Look here, my keys. If anything happen, I want you get in the car and pull off. Don't wait on me, you hear?"

"Yes."

I grabbed my .45 from under the seat, putting it in my waist. I walked up the courtway. Tre walked up to me, dapping me off.

"Nigga, let's do this." We shot the video for *The Dark Side*. This was going to be my new thing. I was going to paint the city red.

The whole Magnolia was in the video; it was live. My girl even got into it. Len was in there too. She kept looking at me crazy. I hadn't been over there in a couple of weeks. So she was tripping.

"That a rap." Bond walked up to me, dapping me off. "Man, that was fire. Look, you got a show in Atlanta. You going open up for *No Limit*."

"Okay, good looking. When?"

"Tomorrow. You need to leave tonight."

"Alright, thanks," I said, dapping him off.

"I'm happy for you," my girl said, kissing me.

"I told I'm trying to get out the streets. Look, go sit in the truck. Let me holla at a few people back here."

"Okay."

I watched as she went and sat in the truck. I walked over to Tre.

"Nigga, that shit was dope," he said, dapping me off.

"Nigga, you want to go out town with me?"

"Fucking right."

"Okay, we leave in the morning."

I went to Len's house, knocking on the door.

"What?"

"Bitch, don't play with me."

"Your ass ain't been back here in a couple weeks."

"I been putting this music shit together."

'Then you bring your girl back here."

"She been coming back here. Don't get to tripping."

"Where my time? I'm the bitch that do whatever it is."

"I'ma go drop my girl off and I'm going to dip back."

"Okay."

I kissed her on the lips.

I ran to my truck, jumped in and pulled off.

***

Slim

When I pulled back up in the projects, my nephew and his crew was sitting on the steps, smoking on blunts, talking to some girls. I walked up on him.

"Nephew, let me holla at you."

"What's up, Uncle."

"Come with me." We walked into my mother's old project. I walked to my room, grabbed the half brick of heroin. I walked back to the kitchen.

"Look, little nigga, I'm about to put you on."

"Okay."

"This a half key of raw. Bring me twenty-five thousand back."

"I got you, Uncle."

"I'm about to go out town. I'm going to holla when I get back."

"I got you, Uncle, he said, dapping me off.

We walked out the apartment. I went to Len's house, knocking on the door.

She answered with some pink boy shorts. I took her ass to the back and bent her over on the dresser, slid my dick into her already wet pussy. I grabbed her by the shoulder, slamming my dick in and out of her as she came all over my dick.

She pushed me on the bed, climbing on top of me, riding me like a pro as I gripped her ass, slamming her down on me as we started coming together.

I jumped up, getting dressed.

"I'm out. I holla when I get back."

Chapter 23

Slim

When I stepped on the stage, the crew went crazy. When I went to performing on my feet, I didn't know motherfuckers know my shit like this. They sang along, rapping my old and new shit.

I had the Centennial Park rocking. Over 30,000 people were there.

I was glad P fucked with a nigga and let nigga open for them. Help a nigga get more exposure.

As I stepped off stage with no shirt on and all my jewelry on, dripping sweat all over my body, I saw a couple bad thick red bones talking to Tre. I walked up and holla at the one with the pink leggings on, with a matching top, and pink and white stiletto boots. Her hair was cut short and dyed yellow. Her girlfriend was thick too. She had black leggings on, a halter top and red stiletto boots. Her hair was black and hung low.

"What up with y'all?" I said.

"Nothing, we like that way you perform."

"What's y'all name?"

"I'm Cookie. My girl here is Lovely."

"What's up? Y'all rolling with us?"

"Yea."

We went straight to the hotel. This was my first time seeing x-pills. Them hoes went to poppin' them. They gave me and Tre one apiece. We popped them and hit some weed. The next thing you know, we was tossing them hoes up.

We took turns fucking both of them. I had Cookie in a doggy style position, fucking her in the ass, while Tre had her friend in the other bed, slamming his dick in her asshole. Then after we bust nut in them hoe, we sat back watching them hoes eat each other out.

We fucked them hoes all night.

***

Kim

I walked outside, jumped in Slim's truck, something I hate doing because you never know what kind of shit he's into. And you never know who want to kill his ass. But I need to go to the store. And my car was in the shop.

I don't know why I stay around fucking with him knowing that he will never change. My friends and family always asking me that same shit. They tell me I can do better. And I agree, but I'm in love with him. I been with him seven years. I know the nigga cheating on me. But it's hard starting over with somebody new.

At least I know what I'm going to get from him. Good dick, money and a lot of stress out night. But one thing for sure: I don't have to worry about him going up side my head and beating on me. All I want from him is a kid, and to get married. A bitch is getting up there. I'm about to turn thirty in a couple months. If he can give me a marriage and a baby, I'll deal with the rest of the shit.

As I was waiting for the light to change on Tchoupitoulas and Napoleon Ave by the Walmart, a black mustang with dark tinted window and black rims pulled up on the side of me. The window came down with a gun sticking out of it.

I just froze up, scared, about to shit and piss on myself.

"Bitch! Pull the window down," he said.

I slowly rolled it down, scared to look at him. I turned and saw a guy with dreads and tattoos over his face.

"Bitch, you're lucky. But tell your nigga I'm looking for him. Tell him Wayne out the St. Thomas on his fucking line."

I was nervous with my head fucked up as he pulled off. I pulled the car over with my hands sweating, my mind fucked up. I began crying.

I don't know what do.

I think I piss on myself.

When I made it home, I slowly got out the truck, going inside, getting in the bed, balling up crying.

***

Slim

The tour was live. I was going to stay with them until the end, but my girl kept calling. At first, I ignored her because I thought she was on some bullshit. But when I checked the voice mail, it sound like some serious shit was going on.

"Hello," I said.

"Where you at?"

"You already know I'm on tour with P."

"You need to come home," she said, crying.

"What's going on?"

"Please come home."

"Tell me what's up."

"Just come home."

Then the phone went dead.

"Shit!" I got off the phone with a thousand thoughts going through my head. I hope a nigga wasn't holding my girl hostage. I got off the tour in the next city. I took a flight and made home in an hour.

When I walked through door, the lights were off.

"Kim! Kim!" I said, with my gun in hand.

She didn't say a word.

When I walked in the room, she was balled up in the bed with the small .38 I gave her.

"Kim! Kim." I said.

I slowly walked over to her. "Kim, what's going on?"

She slowly moved, getting up with the gun in her hand. I just stared at her. Her hair was all over her head, and she looked spook like she seen a ghost.

"Baby, what going on?"

Then she snapped out of it. "Some fucking guy pulled up on me at the fucking light with a gun, said I was lucky that I wasn't you."

"What the fuck!"

"Some nigga named Wayne."

"Okay, it going to be alright. I'm sorry you had to go through that. I'm here now."

"No, it not okay, they want to kill you."

"I got it handled."

I walked up to her, hugging her tight, taking the gun out her hand as she cried on my shoulder. "I'm here now. I got you. Ain't nothing about to happen to you."

I led her on the bed, tongue-kissing her. "Baby, I don't want you to do anything stupid," she said.

"I'm not."

"You promise?"

"Yes." I took her clothes off, laid her back on the bed and went down on her, eating her pussy out.

"Yes, baby, I'm coming," she said, with her legs shaking.

I rose up, sliding my dick into her wet pussy wall as she shook some more, coming back to back. "Slim, I love you," she said, shaking out of control with tears coming down her face.

"I love you too." I came all in her.

About an hour later, she was asleep on my chest as I had a million thoughts going through mind.

I can't let this nigga get away with this shit. Fuck a recording deal. This nigga disrespected my girl. I'm about to fuck this nigga up.

I got dressed in all black, with my all-black hoody.

I grabbed the chopper out the closet.

I jumped in the truck, smashing out on the hunt for this fuck nigga.

Today was Saturday. I know where this nigga like to floss at around the fucking club stunting for hoes.

I rode around a few clubs uptown. I didn't see him.

I know what kind of car he drives; it was a gold Lexus.

Then I rode around *Escape*— this club where somebody always getting killed around here. *Escape* is a club in the 6th Ward that be poppin' on Saturday.

Just then I spotted his car. He was talking to a few bitches; they were leaning on his car. I parked the truck under the bridge. I crept out the truck almost until I got to his car. He didn't even see it coming.

When I raised my gun, it was too late for him to react; I let the chopper ring. I shot him all in the face and body.

Blood went everywhere, with bullets piercing him and his car. People were running and screaming. I ran with them, jumped in the truck, pulling off.

I went to the projects. I put the chopper in my mother's house. Then I jumped in the shower, letting the blood wash off me.

Bitch ass nigga thought he could get away with doing my girl that. He must have thought something was soft about me. I'm a motherfucking warrior. That nigga must forgot I'm the one who put his brother in the grave. I got out the shower, walked in the room, hit a line of coke and dope. I left my mother's house.

I got in the bed with Kim, kissed her and laid next to her like nothing happened. I was thinking about the nigga I just killed.

Robert Baptiste

Chapter 24

Slim

Summer 1995: June

Album Release Party

I pulled up to the club called *Mr. B's*. It was a bar where people in the city come to party, throw events and club. I was throwing my album release party there. The album was coming out tomorrow.

My two singles—*Slippin'* and *You Got It*—were poppin' all over. It was an all-white party.

The whole city showed up for a nigga. The line was wrapped around the corner. Bitches and niggas was showing out for me. I stepped out the truck, dressed in my favorite Girbauds with the Saint's jersey on and black Reeboks. I had the black rag around my neck. And you know I had that .357 on me. Never leave the house without some type of gun.

I walked through the lines. Some of the hoes grabbed on my hands. I brought some them in the club with me.

When I walked in the club, it was packed from wall to wall with the whole Magnolia and uptown. Even a few niggas and hoes from downtown was in this bitch. They had my rap playing, a bandanna hanging up reading: *Slim Album Release Party—The Dark Side*. I walked on the stage in there and performed a little.

When I came off, niggas dapped and hoes hugged.

"Nigga, you made it. I'm proud of you," Tre said.

"Thanks, my nigga. But I'm going to get better. This just the beginning."

"For sure."

"Baby, I'm proud of you." Kim kissed me.

"Thanks, love."

The rest of my hoes came up to me, hugging me. From Len, Tracy and Bam. I told them hoes if they were going to come, my girl was going to be there; so if they couldn't control themselves there, stay the fuck home.

I took pictures with a lot of people. Everything went smooth. No fighting or shooting. It was love in the air.

Chapter 25

Three Weeks Later

Slim

Tre and I was riding down town in the 7th Ward on St. Bernard Street. We pulled at Hunter's Field at the Super Sunday with our straps on our laps. The Super Sunday happen every weekend or every two weeks—sometimes downtown or uptown all across the city. Sometimes it happen across the street from the Magnolia at Shakespeare Park.

They have Indians out second line with people from all over the city. Niggas be out there with their bikes, cars and trucks on chrome rims, stunting for the hoes.

Some niggas be here showing off their pit bulls. Hoes be out there trying to catch ballers niggas by wearing tight clothes or shorts that be riding up in their pussy and having all their ass out, with their hair fixed.

A nigga like me and Tre be trying to catch niggas we beefing with and smoke their ass.

I pulled my truck on the neutral ground, and Tre pulled his car next to mine under the Claiborne Bridge. We stepped out to see what we could see, posting up on my truck with our guns in our waist. Just then, a couple females walked past us. One was high yellow with some yellow leggings on and the matching halter top, with some white Air Maxs on. Her hair was cut short and dyed yellow. The other chick was light-brown with some tight blue shorts on, a black polo shirt and white Reeboks. Her hair was cut short and dyed red.

Both of them hoes was thick as peanut butter. They looked like strippers with the fake nails and tattoos.

I grabbed the yellow, and Tre was on the other one.

"What's up with you?" I said, grabbing the yellow chick by her hand, pulling her to me.

"Nothing, Slim. When you coming out with a new single I can

twerk my ass to?" she said, smiling.

"You know it's coming. What your name?"

"Money."

"*Money*, huh?"

"Yea, that what I'm on."

"Well, let me get your number so I can hit you up."

"You got that," she said, putting her number in my phone.

"I'ma hit your fit ass up tonight," I said, smiling, showing her all my golds.

"You better."

They both walked off, smiling, looking back at us checking their asses out.

They even put a little more twist in it. "Nigga, I'm going to fuck yellow bone tonight," I said.

"You need to because I'm damn sure going to fuck her friend."

As we were coolin', leaning on the truck, we saw this nigga—Dirty—and some of them niggas out the 10th Ward passing in their cars, booting up. We up our guns and went to hitting at them.

People ran and screamed. Dirty and his goons maneuvered their cars, and few lost no time in hitting back at us. We exchanged fire for a couple of minutes. Then the police arrived. We jumped in our shit, smashing out.

The police got behind me. I hit a few corners, throwing the gun out the window. But as soon as I turned by the Lafayette Projects, the police had a road block waiting on me. They jumped out with their guns drawn, pointing at my car.

"Get the fuck out the car now, motherfucker," the police said.

"Fuck!" I said to myself, hitting the steering wheel.

I got out the truck slowly with my hands in the air. They rushed me, putting their knees in my back, and placed handcuffs on me, reading me my rights.

They placed me in the back of the police car, and they reached my truck for guns and drugs. I know they were going to find a half blunt and a needle of heroin in the glove box. I was tripping. I would rather go to jail for drug possession over a gun. As the police drove me to Central Lockup, I thought about this motherfucker probation hold I had on me. I was due to see this motherfucker in a couple months. I was surprised I don't have probation warrant out for my arrest.

When I walked into Central Lockup, this bitch named Joy—whom I use to fuck out the 17th Ward Holly Grove—was working behind the counter.

"Damn! Slim, you just came home," she said.

"Shit, you know how this goes, as long I'm on paper I'm going to stay in and out of this motherfucker. What they charging me with?"

"Shooting in public, drugs and you have a bench warrant for a probation violation."

"Okay, hurry up and process me so I can get upstairs and get something to eat."

She put an orange band on me.

"Where I'm going?"

"H.O.D." She gave me a blanket, cup, soap, and tooth brush. I stepped off the elevator and she walked me over this redbone who was working the floor. "Here." She gave my card to the C.O. " I'ma holla at you later, Slim."

"Be cool."

"Come on," the C.O. said.

I followed the fat chubby chick to the north side. She opened the iron gate, calling for the tier to come to the iron bars.

A brown-skinned nigga with a low, wavy haircut came to the bar.

"Ken Stevenson, you got somebody new coming on your tier."

"Girl, what I told you about calling my whole name."

"Boy, whatever."

"You know I'm digging on you, Ms. Butler."

"Boy, stop, all them hoes coming to see you. Please."

"That's how you going to play me."

"Look, where you putting Slim?"

"Come on, Slim. He going in gate three."

"Okay," she said.

"You going to let me out so I can cut niggas hairs on the floor?"

"I'm going to see," she said, closing the gate and door.

I followed Ken to the last cell, where they had a few niggas I know from different parts of the city. I was glad I didn't see none of my enemies.

But it wasn't like I was tripping on it either. I got a good fighting game.

I walked over to the bunk Y, putting my stuff on it.

"Look, Slim," Ken began, "I cut hair and everything on the tier. I'm on the tier. If you need anything, just holla at me."

"Where you from?" I asked.

"The cut off."

"Okay, I know a few niggas from over there."

"That's what's up. Holla at me," he said, dapping me off, walking out, closing the gate.

I walked over to the phone, calling my girl."

"This is Slim."

"Hello," she said.

"Man, I'm in jail."

"I know, I seen the shit on the news."

"Man, they ain't got shit on me."

"So what your bond?"

"I got a probation hold on me."

"I know that. I kept telling your ass to go see him."

"Look, don't trip on that. Just put some money on my books and go get my truck out the pound."

"Okay. What you think you looking at?"

"I don't know yet."

"Okay, I got you. I'm going to hold you down as always."

"Okay, tell my mother to give you some money. So you can go get my truck."

"Okay, love you."

"Love you back."

***

Slim

Two weeks later, I was sitting in the visitation booth, looking at this white probation officer going through my files. They had dropped the drug possession charges. I was just being held on a probation warrant this bitch ass P.O. was trying to place on me.

"Mr. Morrison, I see they drop the drug charges."

"Yea."

"But you was also charged with discharging a fire arm in public."

"They drop that too. No evidence."

"Yes, they did."

"So why you not letting me go?"

"Well, just because the charges got drop don't mean you didn't do it."

"Whatever."

"Well, on top of that, you haven't been to see me in a couple months."

"Okay, let's get this shit over with. I got to go see rap city."

"Well, I'm going to violate you and give you nine months."

I looked at him and walked out.

When I make on the tier, Ken came up to me. "What happen?"

"Bitch ass nigga give me nine months."

"They might send you up state."

"I hope they do." I walked in the cell, and called my girl.

"Hello," she said.

"Bitch ass nigga give me nine months."

"Okay, I'm here. Love you."

"Love you back."

Robert Baptiste

Chapter 26

Tre

I was riding around uptown in my car, trying to see if I could creep down on one of them fuck niggas out the St. Thomas. They got my nigga back town on a fucking probation hold, where he can't even bond out.

Just then, my phone rang.

"Slim here."

"Whoa, nigga, what's up with you?"

"Nigga, you know I'm coolin' like a big dog suppose to."

"What they give you?"

"Nine months."

"Damn! My nigga, I'm going to hold shit down out here.

"Man, how about your hoe back there?"

"Which one?"

"The bitch Trina."

"Oh. She's cool."

"Man, throw that bitch something and let that hoe drop a package off to a nigga."

"What you talking?"

"Cell phone and ounce of dope. A nigga be sick in this bitch."

"Say no more. I got you. I just drop two hundred on your books."

Good looking out."

"Later."

"Later."

I pulled up in mid-city at this bitch Trina house. I come through and fuck on the bitch from time to time. The hoe be on my dick like mad. I threw her something on her bills and kids.

I walked up to her door, knocking on it. She opened, wearing blue shorts and a white wife beater, her black hair hanging.

She was brown-skinned, a little on the chubby side and cute with some shapely titties that she love for me to suck on.

"What do your red ass want?" she said, with an attitude.

"I need you do me a favor."

"Boy, you tripin', you ain't been over here to see me in a month. Now you need me to do something for you. Boy, you better get the fuck—"

"Damn! Why you tripin' on a nigga?"

"What? Boy, please, bye."

"That's how you going to do me?"

"Yep. That's how you been treating me, running around and fucking these hoes in the city. You ain't been serving me up."

"Why you think I'm here?"

"Don't play with me."

"Are your kids in?"

"Their dad came for them yesterday. They're spending the rest of the week with him."

I grabbed her by the arm, pulling her in the house, pulling her shorts off. She usually don't wear panties, so I was glad to see her naked ass. I pulled out my dick.

"Boy, stop!"

I bent her over on the couch and slid my dick up in her.

"Boy, stop! Boy, stop!" she said, looking back at me, biting her bottom lip.

I grabbed her by the shoulders, slamming my dick deeper in her pussy as she came all over my dick. This what she liked, this rush shit. I slapped her on the ass as I fingered her asshole. I pulled my dick out and slid in her asshole as she back up on me.

"Yes, daddy, fuck me. I miss you."

"I miss you too, Trina."

Moments later, I sat on the couch as she rode my dick with her asshole in a reverse cowgirl position. "I'm about to nut," I said, gripping her waist.

"Shoot that hot cum in my ass," she said, looking back at me, grinding harder. I shook and came all in her ass. We sat back, sweating, trying to catch our breath. "Fuck! I really needed that dick," she said, getting up, walking to the bathroom.

I went into the other bathroom to clean up.

She came back thirty minutes later, wearing a robe with a

towel draped over her head, sitting next to me, smoking on a blunt. "So what you need me to do?"

"Bring this ounce dope and this cell phone to Slim."

"That nigga back in jail."

"On some beef shit."

"I been hearing about y'all beefing with the St. Thomas. Your ass need to be careful. You still fucking with Sharon?"

"Yes, you know that my girl."

"Whatever, nigga. I'm your bitch while you here. And I need five hundred for these."

"Where that nigga you fucking?"

"Nigga, don't play with me."

"Here," I said, giving her a stack.

"Thanks, I need this."

"I'ma dip."

"No, we ain't finish. I need my pussy ate."

I just smiled. As she leaned back, busting her legs open, I went down on her, eating her out until she was shaking convulsively and screaming my name.

***

Slim

I was sitting on the ice cooler in front of the TV when Trina came to bars, calling my name.

"Look out, Slim."

I walked to the bars in shower slippers and PJ's with a black bandanna around my neck. I pushed the gate open and walked out. We walked in the hallway mop closet.

"Here."

'Good looking out," I said, stuffing the bag in my boxers and walked out. I walked back on the tier, going straight to the cell. I put the blanket up over my bed so nobody could see in there. I opened the package and dialed Tre's number.

"Hello," he said.

"I got that. Good looking out."

"Ain't nothing. I drop two hundred on your books."

"A'ight, my nigga, keep your head up. I'll be out there soon. I got these nine months. I hope they let me do it down here."

"That's what's up. Holla if you need anything."

"A'ight, later."

I opened the gram of dope. I made me a line and snorted it. "Fuck! This shit is good," I said, laying back in the bed, loaded as a motherfucker.

I got up about 10 o'clock in the morning. I heard a female voice calling my name. At first, I thought I was tripping. But then this hoe flashed a light on me. I looked up; it was my bitch—Bam. I got up, and walked to the gate.

She opened the gate. I walked out into the hallway.

"What's good?" I asked.

"How much time you got to do?"

'About nine months."

"So what you need from me?"

"To bring some stuff in here."

"Nigga, you ain't fucked me in years."

"So it like that?"

"What you going to give me if I bring in the stuff." She smiled.

"What you want?"

"Let's go in the closet."

She pulled down her pants as I spread her cheeks. I slid my hard dick in her wet pussy, gripping her shoulders, and thrust in and out of her. I stuck my finger in her asshole as she came back to back on my dick.

"Fuck! Yea, daddy, give it to me. I'm coming."

I slammed my dick hard, deeper and fast in her pussy. She backed her ass up on me, bouncing, coming.

"I'm about to nut," I said, shaking. Before long, I shot hot nut in her pussy.

"Damn! Nigga, you still got some good dick," she said, pulling up her pants.

"Bring me some weed, dope, coke and phone."
"I got you."

Robert Baptiste

Chapter 27

Slim

Nine Months Later

1996

I sat in the holding tank, waiting for these bitches to call my name to roll out this motherfucker. These motherfuckers quick to lock you in this motherfucker but be slow to let a nigga go.

These been the longest nine months. I don't know why. Maybe because I was anxious to get back to the free world and lay these raps down I'd been writing in here. My girl been sitting out there in her car since 12:01 midnight. I know she mad as fuck because it's almost two a.m.

"Mr. Brown, pack your shit," the C.O. said.

"Man, I'm ready." I left all my stuff to my home boy. The only thing I took with me was my girl naked pictures. I walked out the holding tank, got my money, and the C.O. cut the arm band off my wrist.

I pushed the door open. The night air hit me, smelling so good. My girl was posted up on her white Lexus car. I walked up to her, hugging and kissing her.

"Baby, I miss you." She smiled.

"I miss you too." We got in the car, pulling off.

As soon as we hit the bedroom door, clothes went flying everywhere. I pushed her on the bed, going down on her, eating her pussy out until she came all in my face. Then she sucked on my dick and balls until I came all in her mouth.

I fucked the shit out of her like DMX did Kisha in *Belly*.

I came hard and fast as she came all over my dick.

"Fuck! Boy, I love you so much."

***

Slim

I sat in the P.O.'s office as he went through the paper work. "You got a job?"

"No."

"You needed to be looking for one."

"I rap for a living."

"Rap? You're a rapper?"

I pulled out my CD and threw it on his desk.

He looked at the CD. "Slim."

"Yea, that my name."

"Okay, I guess you trying to be like this 2Pac guy."

"Or better."

"You think this rap shit really going to get you somewhere?"

"Yea, it might 'cause the streets going to get me dead or in jail."

"Well, I think you still need to get a job. A real one."

"Man, I hear you. Is that all?"

"You still stay in the Magnolia projects?"

"Yea, that my home for years."

"Okay, well, I'm not coming over there. Heard they got a lot of killing back there."

"Yea, and they don't like white in my neighborhood. They think y'all the—"

"Well, can you piss now?"

"Yea."

I pulled out my dick, acting like I was peeing inside the container, whereas it was already filled with my girl's piss.

"Here you go."

He looked at the container. "You got the forty-five dollars?"

I dig in my pocket and give him 50.

"Next month."

I walked out, jumped in my truck, grabbed the needle out the glove box, shooting me some dope and then I pulled the blunt out the ashtray, lighting it, pulling off and blasting 2Pac's *Death Around the Corner*.

I sat in the Magnolia on the porch, ducking, trying to sell these dope bags with my gun on my lap.

Len came out the house, and helped me inside. I sat on her couch with slob coming from my mouth, feeling good.

Robert Baptiste

Chapter 28

Slim

I walked out the booth, listening to the track, as Bond played it back for me. I sat in the chair, fired up a blunt while taking in the rap I just split.

"Man, that shit fire," my nephew said, walking in, giving me a dapp and hug.

"What's up, Nephew?"

"Coolin'. When you got out?"

"A couple days ago."

"Okay, let me jump on this track."

"Go for it."

I sat in there listening to my nephew flow over the track. He was dropping it like it's smoking hot. Just then, Tre hit my phone.

"Nigga, what you got going on?"

"Sitting outside the studio."

"Come holla at me."

I walked outside and jumped in his car. He pulled off, driving around the city as we talked. "What's good?"

"Nigga, I got a lick for us in the 9th Ward."

"What it on?"

"Dope and money."

"Say, bro, you know I'm about that!"

"Well, I'm going to hit you up tonight."

"That's what's up."

He dropped me back off at the studio, and I got in my truck, pulled the needle out the glove box and shot it in my arm.

I walked back in the studio, going back in the booth, splitting some more rap over a couple more track, high as a motherfucker. Once I was through with splitting the rap, I walked back out the booth, and sat down smoking some more.

"So what Hype talking about?"

"Your album don't do good," Bond said.

"What it do?"

"Fifty thousand."

"Damn! That's it?"

"Nigga, you was supposed to be out here to promote the shit!" Bond said.

"Damn! I thought a nigga could still sell a hundred thousand."

"Nah, the music business don't work like that. You got to be out—"

"Whatever. Where my money?"

He gave me a check for thirty-five thousand."

"That's it?"

"Yea, everything come out."

"Man, this rap shit bullshit."

"Yea, if you not going be focus on it."

"Man, I can make more than this shit robbing and selling dope in the—"

Slim, you got to take it more seriously."

"Man, look, music is what I do. Being a street nigga is who I'm. I'm out this bitch."

I jumped in the truck, pulling off, smoking on a blunt.

***

Slim

Later on that night, we pulled up to a red brick house in the low 9th Ward across the canal on Louisa Street. We watched as junkies ran in and out as they got served. We jumped out with the choppers in our hands, running up to the house, pushing the junkies out the way. I shot the first nigga at the door. Tre shot the girl and the other nigga sitting on the couch. I shot the other nigga that was trying to run. I hit him in the head and the back.

I grabbed the bag on the table, loading it up with the money that was stacked on the table while Tre ran through the house, looking for the dope.

Tre came back with two keys of heroin. "Man, they had a door that was locked." We walked up to the door, kicking it in. To our surprise, they had some more money and a key of heroin in there.

We grabbed the shit, stuffing it in the bag. We ran out, jumped in the car, smashing out.

"Nigga! This was a hella lick you put a nigga on."

"Nigga, I told you."

"Nigga, all this money look like a half ticket."

"Shit, I so hope so."

We sat at my mother's house, running the money through the machine. "Nigga, where we at?" I asked.

"Nigga, look like fifty thousand dollars."

"Nigga, it on?"

"You already know."

"For sure."

"Nigga, we already got money over our head. We really going to have money on our shit now."

"Nigga, we got to just stay on our shit. We can't get caught slipping," I said, hitting the blunt, passing to him. Then I continued: "Nigga, with my half the money, I got to put some of it into this album and pay for studio time."

"Nigga, as you should. Me, I'm going to ball like a dog as long niggas getting in the city, I'm going to half it."

"Nigga, you don't want more than this shit?" I asked, hitting the blunt.

"Nigga, what the fuck I'm going to do? I don't know how to work."

"Well, I been thinking about opening my own shit."

"Your own label?"

"Yea, nigga, you should partner with me."

"I'll think about it. Right now, I got bills, and I'm going to enjoy this shit. But you should do it."

"Nigga, whatever, pass me my half."

"Here, nigga, one brick of raw and a hundred and fifty thousand dollars." After a pause, he spoke again, passing me a needle full of dope. "Here, nigga."

I shot it in my arm. He did the same in his arm.

"Nigga, I'm out," I said.

"Me too."

I left some of my stash at my mother's house. I walked in Kim's apartment, putting the rest of the money and dope in her venting system. I got in the bed with her fully dressed and fell asleep.

***

Boo

I walked in my dope shop fucked up in the head by what I seen. My best friend, my cousin and his girl was all dead.

I couldn't even recognize them. I walked down the hallway, only to see all the work and a quarter million of my money gone. With another one of my friends laying in a pool of blood in the hallway. I walked in the kitchen; all the heroin was gone along with $100,000 in cash.

I was furious. I couldn't believe a nigga would try me like this. Motherfucker don't know who I'm. They was going to find out today.

I sat on the sofa, looked at my best friend of ten years and my cousin I know my whole life dead. I kissed them on the forehead and walked out the house, calling the police.

"Boss, what you want me to do?" asked Weedy.

"Nothing. I'm about to call my hitter on this."

We jumped in my Bentley coupé and pulled off.

I walked into my house, picked up my phone, calling my hitter. "Hello," he said, answering on the first ring.

"I need you hear ASAP."

"Okay, I'm on my way." I hung up the phone, walked over to the bar in my house, and pulled myself a Jack, drinking it straight. I still couldn't believe that niggas would try me.

"Weedy, I want the word out on the street—two hundred and fifty thousand dollars on these motherfucker responsible."

"I'm on it, boss," he said, walking out.

I paced back and forth on the hard wooden floor, waiting on

my hitter to come to my house.

***

Real

I pulled up to Boo's house in the eastern part of New Orleans on Lake Forest, where there are some big nice houses. Boo and I go way back in the day. We did time in the prison. Before we got out, he put me down on a couple lick and I took a couple hit for him. Now that we up playing for kilos, I been taking hit for him. I'm his right-hand man. He called me when he needed some business handled. When he called me to his house and the way he sounded on the phone, I knew shit was real fuck up.

I walked up to the door, knocking on it. Boo opened it with a bottle of Jack in his hands and eyes bloodshot like he ain't been to sleep in a few days.

"Man, what's up, Real?"

"Nigga, I need to be asking you that."

"Come in."

We sat down in his living room. His house was laid out with marble and wooden floor everywhere.

"What's going on?"

"Nigga, went in the shop and killed my best friend and rob me of three hundred and fifty thousand dollars and couple bricks of heroin."

"Damn! My nigga."

"Look, I want them nigga who did it dead. And their head brought to me."

"Don't worry. I got it handled," I said, standing up, dapping and hugging him.

"A'ight, my nigga."

"Later."

I walked out the house, jumped in my black Range Rover, and pulled off. As I drove around the city, I picked up the cell phone, calling this bitch—Poo. This my bitch I use to fuck with back in the day. She still hungry for a nigga dick. I go through the Calliope and bust her up from time to time. But the hoe be knowing what going on in the streets. I paid the hoe a few dollars to drop this dope dick on her and she tell me everything I need to know.

Chapter 29

Tre

I just finish serving my last bag of dope, and going to get in my truck when my nigga—Will—walked up to me. Will was one of my partners in the project I be front dope to. He was a young pretty boy nigga. He be getting money in the project. Got all the hoe on his dick.

"What's up, my nigga?" I said.

"Man, I need a ride. I left my car by one of my hoes downtown."

"A'ight, come on."

We jumped in my car, pulling off.

"Nigga, what good?" I said.

"Man, you know me fucking these hoes and getting this money. You got something for me?"

"Yea, holla at me later."

"I got you."

As we was sitting waiting for the light to change on Claiborne Ave by Circle Food Store on St. Bernard, we kept talking.

"Man, when you going to hook me up with one of the freaks?" I asked.

"Man, I got you."

As I was about to pull off, a black Range Rover pulled up on the side of me, opening up fire. They went to shooting my truck up. I smashed out, yet they was still hitting at my truck. They shot all the back window out. I looked at Will; he had two holes in his head. I was trying to duck from the shot when I rose up. I tried to turn, but ran into the side of the bridge.

I was dazed up. I heard the nigga coming, so I jumped out the truck even though I was dazed, shooting at them niggas. I stumbled to somebody back yard, hiding under somebody house.

"Damn! Them nigga kill my man." I grabbed my phone, calling my girl.

"Hello."

"Girl, I need you to come get me."

"Okay, where you at?"

"In the 7th Ward around Circle Food Store."

"I'm on my way."

***

Sharon

When I pulled up around there, my heart dropped when I saw his truck smashed into the side of the bridge. I saw the ambulances pulling somebody out of the truck and they was dead. I looked around for Tre, but don't see him. Next thing I know, my phone was rang. "Where are you?"

"By the pink house.

"Alright."

As I pulled up to the house, he ran up to my car, getting in with blood all over him.

"Boy, what the fuck happen?"

"Nothing. Drive."

"Something happen."

"Some nigga rode down on my truck shooting the motherfucker up. They kill my little partner Will."

"Fuck! Man, we need to move out the city. This beef shit out control."

"Girl, just bring me home so I can change my clothes."

"See, that the shit I'm talking about."

"Look, Sharon, not now. I'm not trying to hear that shit. Man got killed and I got blood all over me, please stop!"

At home, I got in the shower, ducking my head under it, letting the blood rinse off me. My face was cut by all the glass poppin' in my face. I don't need stitches. I thought about my man Will. Damn! My nigga got killed over some beef shit of mine. I'm going to get whoever done this. I swear. My thought was broke when Sharon pulled the curtain back, standing there butt ass naked. "Can I come in?"

"Yes,"

She stepped in the shower, tongue-kissing me and stroking my dick. Then she dropped to her knees, sucking my dick. I closed my eyes, enjoying it. Then I carried her, putting her legs on my shoulders, fucking her like crazy, as she dig her nails in my back, and we came together afterwards.

***

Real

"Fuck! Yea, nigga, give me that dick! I love you."

I was hitting this bitch named Poo from the back as I finger-fucked her asshole. Poo was a thick red bone out the Calliope, with short purple hair and dimples.

She been on my dick since she found out I was out here busting head. But the bitch is not to be trusted. That why I got this hoe in the hotel way in Slidell. "Bitch, I'm about to nut," I said, pulling my dick out, shooting my hot come all over her ass and back.

"Fuck! That dope dick is good."

She got out the bed, going to the bathroom. I laid back and lit a blunt.

She came back in the room, getting in the bed with me while I smoked on the blunt.

"Now, tell what you heard in the streets about who robbed Boo house."

Well, I heard it was Slim and Tre out the Magnolia."

"Yea, is that right?"

"Yea, and they got a lot of nigga in the city trying to get the two hundred and fifty thousand dollars on their head. Plus I heard niggas out the St. Bernard and St. Thomas wanting to kill them too."

"Good looking out."

"I need few dollars."

I gave her a stack.

I picked up the phone, hitting Boo up."

"What's up, nigga?"

"I found out who did it."

"Who?"

"The nigga Slim and Tre."

"Handle that."

"I got you."

I got up, getting dressed. "Where you going?" she asked.

"I got to go handle this business."

"Please stay."

"Shit, I'm going to catch up with you. Here, another hundred. Get home."

I grabbed my Mac, walking out, and jumped in my Impala, pulling off. I was heading back to the city on the hunt for these niggas.

Chapter 30

Slim

I woke up the next evening to my phone ringing. I got up, looked at this fine ass hoe Peaches while she was butt naked with her big ass in the air. Damn, I know Kim will have a shit fit because I ain't came home last night. I picked up my phone, looking at the number; it was Tre.

"What's good, my nigga?"

"Man, it all bad."

"What's going on?"

"Man, some nigga rolled up on me in a truck and went blasting."

"What!"

"Yea, and they killed my nigga Will."

"Damn! Who was it?"

"Man, we beefing with so many niggas I couldn't tell who it was."

"You good?"

"Nigga, still shook. I ran my truck in the side of a bridge."

"Where at?"

"In the 7th Ward around Circle Food Store."

"Damn! My nigga, we going to find out who did that shit."

"For sure. Where your ass at?"

"Man, I fell asleep at the house of this fine bitch name Peaches."

"Bitch, Kim going to kill your ass."

"I know. But this hoe is a big freak. I hit this bitch all in her ass."

"That thick black bitch?"

"Yea, my throwback hoe."

"For sure."

"Look, nigga, I'm going to catch up with you later in the project. We going to handle that business."

"Later."

"Later."

I threw on my clothes, grabbed my gun and slapped Peaches on her ass.

"I'm out."

"You leaving?"

"I got to handle some business."

She got up, walking me to the door naked and kissed me. "When you coming back?"

"Later on."

"Okay."

I walked out the hallway, the sun damn near blinding me as I looked both ways before I went to my vehicle. Niggas be jacking back here for real, I had to be extra cautious. I jumped in my truck, smashing out.

***

Slim

Later on that night, we rode around the club called *The Duck Off*. It was located in the 7th Ward. A bunch of niggas out the 7th hanging out there. I know for sure we was going to catch a bunch of them niggas slipping around there.

We had our choppers on our laps, looking for them. My bitch Bam already sent me a picture of Steven and a few niggas he roll with. As we were making a second loop around the club, I spotted some niggas out the St Bernard.

I parked my car two houses down the club. We stepped out, crept down low with the choppers in our hand. Soon, we ran up on them, blasting.

Boom! Boom! Boom!

People began running and ducking.

We jumped back in the truck, pulling off.

"Man, I told we were going to get them."

"For sure," Tre said, snorting dope.

We made our way back to the project, sitting on the steps,

hustling heroin and getting loaded.

Robert Baptiste

Chapter 31

Steven

I was riding around the city, looking for Slim and Tre. Them niggas killed a couple of my niggas at the club last night.

Plus this nigga Jews been on my back about kidnapping these niggas or this bitch Brandy who set his brother up.

As I was coming across Napoleon Ave., I spotted that hoe.

"There that bitch car right there," I said to myself. She was parked at this Walgreen.

I parked in the parking a lot, waiting for her to come out. As she walked to her car, I jumped out with the gun and ran up to her.

"Bitch, if you scream, I'm going to kill you right here in broad day light. Let's go." I put her in my car.

I got in, calling Jews as I pulled off.

"I got her."

"Okay, bring her to the warehouse."

"A'ight."

"Please don't kill me."

We pulled up to the warehouse. I blew the horn, the gate opened up and I said, "Bitch, get out."

"Please don't kill me."

I pushed her out.

"Bitch, get naked."

"What! No," she said, shaking.

"Bitch, do it," I said, pointing the gun to her head.

Crying, she took off her clothes.

Then the crew took turns tossing her up.

Just then, Jews walked in the warehouse with his pit bull.

We pulled our pants up.

He walked over to her, grabbing her hair. "Is this the bitch that set my brother up?"

"Please, I don't know what you talking about."

"Shut the fuck up, you lying bitch!" Jews said, slapping the shit out of her.

Chapter 32

Slim

I was sitting at home watching the TV, loaded as a motherfucker. I had been trying to get in touch with this hoe Brandy. I need a lick. I had been calling the bitch for a couple days now. And the bitch wasn't answering her phone.

Just then, I thought I was tripping when I heard the news call out her name.

"Brandy Green was found dead last night in a dumper. She was shot in the head and raped."

"What the fuck!" I jumped up, my head was fucked up.

The only person who could have did this was this nigga Jews out the Bernard. He had money on all our head. I know he had somebody kidnap her. He was trying to send me a message. I got it loud and clear. I'm about to finish this shit.

I picked up the phone, calling this bitch Peaches. "Hello," she said.

"You see them nigga back there?"

"Who?"

"Jews and Steve."

"Yes, they sitting at the game room right now."

"Okay, I'm on my way around there."

I pulled up in the project with the chopper on my lap.

"Nigga, get in."

"What's up?" Tre asked.

"You got your gun?"

"What's good?"

"Man, them niggas out the St. Bernard kidnapped Brandy, raped her and dumped her body in the dumpers."

"What! How you know that?"

"I seen the shit on the news."

"Okay, let's do this shit."

"I'm going to meet you in the project."

"Let's end this shit."

I picked up Tre and headed to the St. Bernard. I picked up the phone, calling my bitch.

"Hello."

"Them niggas still out there?"

"Yea, they hanging in front the store."

"Okay."

I parked a couple of cars down.

I saw Jews and his crew hanging out talking. We crept down on them. When we up the chopper, we went to busting. They tried to run. Tre shot the nigga Steve in the head. I shot the nigga Dave twice in the back, and Tre shot the other nigga in the back and arm. I ran over to Dave, finishing him. I shot him twice in the face. We ran back to my truck, getting in and smashing out.

Chapter 33

Real

Here I'm riding around, looking for this nigga Slim or Tre. After I fuck the shit out that bitch—Poo—she told me Slim and Tre ran in Boo house.

Then some of my people I talk to heard the same thing. I know it was true. They say them nigga flossing around in new whip and jewelry and pushing a lot of coke. The word get around in New Orleans because it real small. And everybody know everybody. I looked at my watch; it was 11 o'clock. I been from uptown to downtown, looking for these niggas. They duck real good. A thought came to me. I know where I can catch these nigga slipping at. The one place they would least be expecting me to come to was in their projects. Bet I can catch them there. I pulled up in the dark driveway on Thalia. I jumped out with my 9mm in my hand. I walked in the M.L.K Courtway, looked around for them. No sign of them.

I ran in the hallway where dope fiends and crackheads getting high. They ran out when they saw me with the gun in my hand. Then this dumb bitch named Tamikia came out her house. This dumb fat bitch is letting the whole city fuck her even though she got about five kids. She must got some good pussy.

"Boy! Real, what you doing back here? You know them nigga catch you back here, you dead."

I was beefing with a few niggas from back here and uptown, because I killed a couple niggas back here, back in the day; that's what I did ten years for in Angola. My name rang in the city as one of the top killers.

"Man, take your fat ass inside," I answered Tamikia.

"Nigga, who you think you talking to? I'm not scared of you."

If I wasn't already on a mission, I would have smoke this bitch. I don't care who you are, anybody can get it from me— woman, man or child. I don t have no picks.

"You seen Slim or Tre?"

"No. And what you looking for them for?"

"Well, you better know what you doing fucking with them."

"Whatever," she said, going inside.

***

Slim

I was coming out the pizza shop on Decatur by the river. I got a lot of white people I be serving in the French quarter. I been selling coke bags out here when it get slow in the project, plus ounces, quarter and twenty bags double out here.

The pizza spot be poppin' because of the tour. And it boom seven days a week.

I could sell a whole brick out here in two weeks. That's how hard it be jumping out here. They sell any kind drug you want, from weed heroin, pills and coke. The coke game been good to me, but I need to get in the heroin business. Yea, I rap and shit, but that heroin money was where it at. I get my hand on a couple block of that shit, I'm saying fuck the rap game. I hit me line of dope I got from out the St. Thomas. They got that fire back there. I need to get my hand on some of that shit.

I walked out the bathroom, feeling good. I looked at my watch; it was 12:00. I need to go fuck something. Kim was working a double shift at the hospital. Brandy was dead. Len was probably in the project sitting at home waiting for a nigga to come through and bust her up. I'll fuck her in a minute; that where I'm going. Plus I need somebody to drive my truck back from the dealership. I'm about to get my Porsche truck tomorrow, something to floss on them niggas with at the Super Sunday this weekend.

I jumped in my truck, picking up my phone, calling my cousin again. This nigga still ain't hit me back and I hit this nigga like three times already. I'm trying to get some heroin and this nigga got a nice connect in Houston on it.

"This Ken, leave a message."

Damn! The fucking voice mail! "Hey, this your cousin. Hit me back."

I pulled off. As I was pulling up in the project, I heard two shots, then two bullets hit my passenger side door.

Doom! Doom!

"What the fuck!" A nigga shooting at me.

Two more hit the window. I jumped out the truck, pulling my gun off my hip, trying to see where the gunfire was coming from. Then some more shots rang out, hitting my car. I shot back in the direction it was coming from. Then I saw a nigga dressed in all black with a bald head. He was shooting out the hallway. I shot back. We exchanged fire for a second. Then I ran in the hallway when I saw the police coming in the courtway. Somebody must have called them. I stood in the hallway as I watched the police come in the project and surround my car that was shot up.

Damn! A nigga was on my line waiting for me to come in the jets. I need to found out who that fuck that was.

I slid out the courtway, going to Len's house, knocking on her door.

"Who is it?"

"Me."

She opened the door with some white shorts on and a white wife beater. She was barefoot with her hair done.

"Was that you shooting?"

I walked past her, going to the room, and put my gun at the top of the closet with her on my heel. "Yea, somebody was waiting on me to come back here. They shot my truck up."

"What!"

She walked out the room.

I thought to myself, *I need to report my truck stolen so the police won't be on line questioning me about the shooting.* I picked up the phone, called the police, reporting it stolen. She walked back in, smoking on a blunt and sat on my lap.

"You want to hit this? The police still out there going through your truck."

"Yea, let me hit that."

I hit the blunt, rubbing her on the ass as my dick got hard. I was getting high the more I smoked that shit. She stood up, took her shorts off and climbed in the bed, spreading her legs. I took my clothes off, slid my dick in her wet warm pussy, and put her legs on my shoulders and began fucking the shit out of her. She dig her nails into my back, shaking and coming all over my dick.

I got up the next morning. We drove to the police impound first. The police called and said they had found my truck. It had multiple bullet holes in it. And it was totaled. I don't care. I had another on the way. I grabbed my stuff out of it and headed to the dealership. I jumped in my black Porsche truck. It had black leather seats with some other fancy features. It hit a nigga for $75,000.

"Baby, them nigga and hoes ain't going to be able to take you when you show up with this motherfucker," Len said.

"And that how I want. Look, I'm going to meet you back in the project. I got something to handle."

"Alright." She kissed me.

As I pulled off, my phone rang. It was Tre.

"Hey, nigga," he said.

"What good?"

"Man, word on the streets say Boo paid this nigga Real to kill us."

"Yea."

"Yea, thirty hands apiece."

"I think that who was shooting at me last night."

"Damn! My nigga, you got in a shoot-out last night, nigga?"

"Yea, a nigga was waiting on me. And shot my truck up."

"Might been that nigga. You got to watch him. He one of the old killers."

"I'm glad to know that. Now I'm on that nigga line."

"You already know."

"I'm on to holla at you later."

"A'ight."

I drove around, thinking to myself that whoever it was shooting at me, I'm going to get that nigga. Him and Boo. I got nigga all over that city trying to get at me. I don't give a fuck from uptown to downtown niggas put prices on my head and want to see me dead. But they just don't know I'm on their line too. And the first chance I get to catch them slipping, they are dead. So they better be on their job, because I'm not playing no game with these niggas out here.

Robert Baptiste

Chapter 34

Slim

I pulled up at the Super Sunday across from the Magnolia Project at Shakespeare Park. The Super Sunday be all over the city. This time it was uptown.

I was watching the niggas stunting in their cars, trucks, and bikes. And I was watching the hoes with their shorts on with their hair done, trying to fuck a baller nigga.

Tre walked up to me, smoking on a blunt. "What's up, nigga?" he said.

"Nigga, coolin'. Just peeping out which one of niggas I'm going to jack."

"What's up with the rap shit?"

"Man, my shit just sold fifty thousand."

"Damn!"

"Yea, when a nigga went to jail, they don't even promote a nigga shit."

"Damn! I'm sorry to hear that."

"It cool. I'ma do something for myself."

"For sure."

"I just got my money up."

"I feel you. My pocket hurting."

"Mine too."

"We going to come up."

"You already know."

Just then, two fine ass hoes walked past us. One was Poo: this redbone who I been trying to fuck out the Calliope. She had on some red tight shorts, a red BeBe shirt, and white Reeboks. Her hair was cut short and dyed gold with a black tint.

"What's up, Poo?" I said.

"Nothing. What's up, Slim?"

"Trying to holla at you. But you be acting bad with a nigga."

Tre jumped on her friend that was fine and brown-skinned.

"No, I'm not."

"So won't you give your number and let me call you?"
"Look, let me get yours and I'm going to hit you up."
"You must got a man."
"I got friends."
"Okay, you better holla a nigga."
"I got you."

***

Slim

I pulled up to the daiquiri shop in the 17th Ward. It was pack with niggas and hoes from everywhere in the city. You got to be on your P and Q out here because a nigga will try to get at you. It was the same people for Super Sunday. It's a thing for us in the city—go to Super Sunday, the lake, then daiquiri shop.

I stepped out the truck, leaning on it, smoking on a blunt. I was watching the hoes go by. Just like at the Super Sunday, niggas out stunting, showing off the hoes. This very bitch caught my eyes.

She was dark-skinned, short with black hair that came to her shoulders. She had a big round ass that was fitting tight in some red leggings with a matching halter top and some white Nikes. I pulled up on her. "What's up, love? What's your name?"

"Dayton."
"I'm Slim."
"Nice to meet you, Slim?"
"Let me by you a daiquiri."
"Cool."
"So what you doing after this?"
"Nothing, why?"
"Well, I'm trying to see what good."
She just smiled.

As we were standing in the line inside the daiquiri shop, bullets began hitting the windows. I ducked, pulled her down, trying to see where the gunfire was coming from. I saw a couple of niggas out the St. Thomas. I crawled on the floor as them niggas was hitting at me. Then I heard the police.

As I was trying to get out, the police rushed in, slamming me on the ground. They handcuffed me and patted me down, and found the gun I had on me.

"Fuck!" I said.

I sat in the cell in Central Lockup, trying to call the bail bond before they put a probation hold on me.

"Hello," Ray said.

"Man, I need you to come get me ASAP."

"Nigga, what they got you on?"

"A gun. But I'm on probation."

"Okay, nigga, I got you." Mr. Ray is one bail bond that take anything. He was once a big time drug dealer. He finally got his license and started a bail bond company.

I dialed Kim's number.'

"Hello."

"Baby, I'm in jail. I need you to get some money and bring down here."

"Okay. How much?"

"About thirty stack."

"Okay. I'm on the way."

I called Ray back. "How much I need?"

"Twenty-five thousand."

"Okay, I got my girl bringing something."

I was looking over at the niggas in the other holding tank. They were booting me up. Just then the fat black C.O. opened the door, calling my name. I walked out the cell, giving those niggas the finger. I walked behind the C.O., getting processed out. When I walked out, Kim was right there leaning on the white B.M.W I had bought her.

"Hey, baby," I said, walking up to her, kissing her."

"Here, the money."

"Okay. Come on, let's go."

We pulled up at the bail bond place on Tulane and Broad.

Ray looked up when I walked into his office.

"Nigga, you owe me twenty-five grand."

I peeled off twenty-five grand.

"Good looking out," I said as I handed him he cash.

"Nigga, you better not miss your court day. Don't let me have to get them bounty hunter on your ass."

Ray was an older, short black man with a bald head who was an ex-convict. He did twenty years back in the day for drugs. He came home, got his kids to get a license and they opened a bail bonding business with the rest of the money the feds didn't take. So now he help motherfuckers get out of jail. He take everything from jewelry to cars, to your house. You don't pay, he keep it for good.

"I got you," I said, dapping him off before walking out.

Chapter 35

Slim

The DJ had the whole Magnolia rocking. They had hoes and niggas from everywhere back here. I was just chilling on the porch, loaded off that dope and had a blunt in my hand. The project was celebrating Juv song that was about to come out: *Solja Rags*. It had the whole city rocking.

I was still trying to find a nigga I could get. I was low on cash. I had no dope left. A nigga was straight fuck up. I need a lick.

"What's up, nigga?" Tre said.

"Nigga coolin'. Trying to find a lick."

"I know."

As I was blowing the smoke out my nose, my phone rang.

I looked down at it. It was the bitch Poo whom I was trying to fuck.

"What's good?"

"What's up, Slim?"

"Nothing, coolin' in the 'jects."

"Won't you come and pick a bitch up?"

"A'ight. Where you at? I'm on the way."

"By my friend in the 6th Ward."

"A'ight."

"Bye."

"Nigga, I'm out."

"A'ight, fuck with me later. I might have something for us."

"Cool."

I pulled up to her friend house in the 6th Ward, blowing the horn.

She came outside wearing some tight red shorts that was all in her pussy and ass, with a blue and white polo shirt and some white Reeboks. Her hair was pulled back in a ponytail. The bitch was thick just as I remember her.

She jumped in my truck, smelling good as fuck. "Nigga, I wanna smoke something."

"Look in the glove box."

She grabbed the blunt and lit it up, taking a hit and choking. She passed it to me. I hit it and passed it back to her.

I pulled in the Calliope in the J27 driveway.

I grabbed the strap from under the seat.

Even though I fuck with a few niggas back here, you still got be careful 'cause a nigga will still you back here.

We walked in her apartment. She led me to her bedroom and she took off her clothes. Then she unzipped my pants, dropped to her knees and began deep-throating my dick.

She had me with my eyes close tight and my toes curled up. She pushed me on the bed, climbed on top of me and rode my dick like a cow girl, as I gripped her hip while slamming her down on top of me.

"Fuck! This dick is good, Slim." She bit down on her bottom lip, playing with her titties.

I flipped her over, putting here on her back with her legs on my shoulders and her feet touching the head board. I began beasting her out, her legs shaking and her toes curling up.

"Fuck! Don't Stop! I'm coming! Don't stop." She dig her nails into my back.

The deeper I went into her, the more she came all over my dick; it was shooting out like water. I flipped her over into a doggy style position. I grabbed her ass cheeks and slammed my dick in and out of her soaking wet pussy. I began to shake as she backed her ass up on me.

"Fuck! I'm about to nut."

She pulled my dick out her pussy and slid it into her asshole. She slid back on my dick as I thrust in and out of her asshole.

"Fuck! This dick feel good."

I grabbed her ass cheeks tighter, shooting all my nut inside her.

We fell on the bed, trying to catch our breath. "Damn! Slim, you fuck me some good." She got up, going into her bathroom while I dig in my pocket pulling out a bag of dope, snorting it.

***

Real

I rode around the city, looking for these niggas. Because this nigga Boo been on my line about killing these niggas after I told him who rob his dope house. He gave me $30,000 up front and the rest was going to come when I finish the job. But the bad part was: Boo got the whole city on these niggas line so anybody can cash in.

I convinced the bitch Poo to set this nigga up after she told me he holla at her at the daiquiri shop. The bitch don't want to do it at first, but I gave her ten grand. It had been a couple of days and the bitch ain't hit me. I hope the bitch don't change her mind. Because I was going to smoke her ass too if she was playing game.

As I was snorting a line of dope, the bitch called my phone.

"What's good?"

"This nigga is sleeping at my house in the project right now."

"Alright. I'm on my way."

***

Slim

I got up out the bed and looked at the clock; it read 4 in the morning. I looked at the bitch; she was knocked out. I grabbed my clothes, put them on, grabbed my gun and head out the door.

As I was coming out the dark hallway, going to my truck, with my gun under my arm, all I saw was a shadow come from behind the dumper, shooting at me. I felt the hot bullets rip through my clothes, hitting me in my chest, arms and legs. I fell back against my truck and slid down.

The only thing I remember hearing was Bond saying you can't have one foot in the streets and one foot out. Damn, he was right. This nigga caught me slipping, then everything went black.

***

Real

"What the fuck! Shit!" I said, looking at all the police and ambulance out there. I backed up out the driveway, smashing out, thinking to myself: *What the fuck happen that quick? I was just down the street in the Magnolia. Don't tell me a nigga got this nigga first.*

"Shit, there goes half the money! I need find this bitch ass nigga Tre. So I can get the rest of the money."

Just then, my phone rang. It was Poo. "Hello."

"Bitch, what kind of game you playing?"

"Nigga, what the fuck you talking about?"

"Bitch, they got all kind of police in your driveway."

"Wasn't that you who killed the nigga?"

"Fuck no."

"Well, somebody did."

I hung up. "Ain't this a bitch."

To Be Continued…
The Streets Never Let Go 2
Coming Soon

Submission Guideline

Submit the first three chapters of your completed manuscript to ldpsubmissions@gmail.com, subject line: Your book's title. The manuscript must be in a .doc file and sent as an attachment. Document should be in Times New Roman, double spaced and in size 12 font. Also, provide your synopsis and full contact information. If sending multiple submissions, they must each be in a separate email.

Have a story but no way to send it electronically? You can still submit to LDP/Ca$h Presents. Send in the first three chapters, written or typed, of your completed manuscript to:

LDP: Submissions Dept
Po Box 944
Stockbridge, Ga 30281

DO NOT send original manuscript. Must be a duplicate.

Provide your synopsis and a cover letter containing your full contact information.

Thanks for considering LDP and Ca$h Presents.

NEW RELEASES

FRIEND OR FOE 3 by MIMI
A GANGSTA'S KARMA by FLAME
NIGHTMARE ON SILENT AVE by CHRIS GREEN
THE STREETS MADE ME 3 by LARRY D.
WRIGHT
MOBBED UP 3 by KING RIO
JACK BOYZ N DA BRONX 3 by ROMELL TUKES
A DOPE BOY'S QUEEN 3 by ARYANNA
MOB TIES 3 by SAYNOMORE
CONFESSIONS OF A GANGSTA by NICHOLAS
LOCK
MURDA WAS THE CASE by ELIJAH R. FREEMAN
THE STREETS NEVER LET GO by ROBERT BAP-
TISTE

Coming Soon from Lock Down Publications/Ca$h Presents
BLOOD OF A BOSS **VI**

SHADOWS OF THE GAME II

TRAP BASTARD II

By **Askari**

LOYAL TO THE GAME **IV**

By **T.J. & Jelissa**

IF TRUE SAVAGE **VIII**

MIDNIGHT CARTEL IV

DOPE BOY MAGIC IV

CITY OF KINGZ III

NIGHTMARE ON SILENT AVE II

By **Chris Green**

BLAST FOR ME **III**

A SAVAGE DOPEBOY III

CUTTHROAT MAFIA III

DUFFLE BAG CARTEL VII

HEARTLESS GOON VI

By **Ghost**

A HUSTLER'S DECEIT III

KILL ZONE II

BAE BELONGS TO ME III

By **Aryanna**

COKE KINGS V

KING OF THE TRAP III

By **T.J. Edwards**

GORILLAZ IN THE BAY V

3X KRAZY III

De'Kari

KINGPIN KILLAZ IV

STREET KINGS III

PAID IN BLOOD III

CARTEL KILLAZ IV

DOPE GODS III

Hood Rich

SINS OF A HUSTLA II

ASAD

RICH $AVAGE II

By Troublesome

YAYO V

Bred In The Game 2

S. Allen

CREAM III

By Yolanda Moore

SON OF A DOPE FIEND III

HEAVEN GOT A GHETTO II

By Renta

LOYALTY AIN'T PROMISED III

By Keith Williams

I'M NOTHING WITHOUT HIS LOVE II

SINS OF A THUG II

TO THE THUG I LOVED BEFORE II

By Monet Dragun

QUIET MONEY IV

EXTENDED CLIP III

THUG LIFE IV

By **Trai'Quan**

THE STREETS MADE ME IV

By **Larry D. Wright**

IF YOU CROSS ME ONCE II

By **Anthony Fields**

THE STREETS WILL NEVER CLOSE II

By **K'ajji**

HARD AND RUTHLESS III

THE BILLIONAIRE BENTLEYS II

Von Diesel

KILLA KOUNTY II

By **Khufu**

MOBBED UP IV

By **King Rio**

MONEY GAME II

By **Smoove Dolla**

A GANGSTA'S KARMA II

By **FLAME**

JACK BOYZ VERSUS DOPE BOYZ

By **Romell Tukes**

MOB TIES IV

By **SayNoMore**

MURDA WAS THE CASE II

Elijah R. Freeman

THE STREETS NEVER LET GO II

By **Robert Baptiste**

<u>**Available Now**</u>

RESTRAINING ORDER **I & II**

By **CA$H & Coffee**

LOVE KNOWS NO BOUNDARIES **I II & III**

By **Coffee**

RAISED AS A GOON I, II, III & IV

BRED BY THE SLUMS I, II, III

BLAST FOR ME I & II

ROTTEN TO THE CORE I II III

A BRONX TALE I, II, III

DUFFLE BAG CARTEL I II III IV V VI

HEARTLESS GOON I II III IV V

A SAVAGE DOPEBOY I II

DRUG LORDS I II III

CUTTHROAT MAFIA I II

KING OF THE TRENCHES

By **Ghost**

LAY IT DOWN **I & II**

LAST OF A DYING BREED I II

BLOOD STAINS OF A SHOTTA I & II III

By **Jamaica**

LOYAL TO THE GAME I II III

LIFE OF SIN I, II III

By **TJ & Jelissa**

BLOODY COMMAS I & II

SKI MASK CARTEL I II & III

KING OF NEW YORK I II,III IV V

RISE TO POWER I II III

COKE KINGS I II III IV

BORN HEARTLESS I II III IV

KING OF THE TRAP I II

By **T.J. Edwards**

IF LOVING HIM IS WRONG…I & II

LOVE ME EVEN WHEN IT HURTS I II III

By **Jelissa**

WHEN THE STREETS CLAP BACK I & II III

THE HEART OF A SAVAGE I II III

By **Jibril Williams**

A DISTINGUISHED THUG STOLE MY HEART I II & III

LOVE SHOULDN'T HURT I II III IV

RENEGADE BOYS I II III IV

PAID IN KARMA I II III

SAVAGE STORMS I II

AN UNFORESEEN LOVE

By **Meesha**

A GANGSTER'S CODE I &, II III

A GANGSTER'S SYN I II III

THE SAVAGE LIFE I II III

CHAINED TO THE STREETS I II III

BLOOD ON THE MONEY I II III

By J-Blunt

PUSH IT TO THE LIMIT

By **Bre' Hayes**

BLOOD OF A BOSS **I, II, III, IV, V**

SHADOWS OF THE GAME

TRAP BASTARD

By **Askari**

THE STREETS BLEED MURDER **I, II & III**

THE HEART OF A GANGSTA I II& III

By **Jerry Jackson**

CUM FOR ME I II III IV V VI VII

An **LDP Erotica Collaboration**

BRIDE OF A HUSTLA **I II & II**

Robert Baptiste

THE FETTI GIRLS **I, II& III**

CORRUPTED BY A GANGSTA I, II III, IV

BLINDED BY HIS LOVE

THE PRICE YOU PAY FOR LOVE I, II ,III

DOPE GIRL MAGIC I II III

By **Destiny Skai**

WHEN A GOOD GIRL GOES BAD

By **Adrienne**

THE COST OF LOYALTY I II III

By Kweli

A GANGSTER'S REVENGE **I II III & IV**

THE BOSS MAN'S DAUGHTERS I II III IV V

A SAVAGE LOVE **I & II**

BAE BELONGS TO ME I II

A HUSTLER'S DECEIT I, II, III

WHAT BAD BITCHES DO I, II, III

SOUL OF A MONSTER I II III

KILL ZONE

A DOPE BOY'S QUEEN I II III

By **Aryanna**

A KINGPIN'S AMBITON

A KINGPIN'S AMBITION **II**

I MURDER FOR THE DOUGH

By **Ambitious**

TRUE SAVAGE I II III IV V VI VII

DOPE BOY MAGIC I, II, III

MIDNIGHT CARTEL I II III

CITY OF KINGZ I II

NIGHTMARE ON SILENT AVE

By **Chris Green**

The Streets Never Let Go

A DOPEBOY'S PRAYER

By **Eddie "Wolf" Lee**

THE KING CARTEL **I, II & III**

By **Frank Gresham**

THESE NIGGAS AIN'T LOYAL **I, II & III**

By **Nikki Tee**

GANGSTA SHYT **I II &III**

By **CATO**

THE ULTIMATE BETRAYAL

By **Phoenix**

BOSS'N UP **I , II & III**

By **Royal Nicole**

I LOVE YOU TO DEATH

By **Destiny J**

I RIDE FOR MY HITTA

I STILL RIDE FOR MY HITTA

By **Misty Holt**

LOVE & CHASIN' PAPER

By **Qay Crockett**

TO DIE IN VAIN

SINS OF A HUSTLA

By **ASAD**

BROOKLYN HUSTLAZ

By **Boogsy Morina**

BROOKLYN ON LOCK I & II

By **Sonovia**

GANGSTA CITY

By **Teddy Duke**

A DRUG KING AND HIS DIAMOND I & II III

A DOPEMAN'S RICHES

Robert Baptiste

HER MAN, MINE'S TOO I, II
CASH MONEY HO'S
THE WIFEY I USED TO BE I II
By Nicole Goosby
TRAPHOUSE KING **I II & III**
KINGPIN KILLAZ I II III
STREET KINGS I II
PAID IN BLOOD **I II**
CARTEL KILLAZ I II III
DOPE GODS I II
By **Hood Rich**
LIPSTICK KILLAH **I, II, III**
CRIME OF PASSION I II & III
FRIEND OR FOE I II III
By **Mimi**
STEADY MOBBN' **I, II, III**
THE STREETS STAINED MY SOUL I II
By **Marcellus Allen**
WHO SHOT YA **I, II, III**
SON OF A DOPE FIEND I II
HEAVEN GOT A GHETTO
Renta
GORILLAZ IN THE BAY **I II III IV**
TEARS OF A GANGSTA I II
3X KRAZY I II
DE'KARI
TRIGGADALE I II III
MURDAROBER WAS THE CASE
Elijah R. Freeman
GOD BLESS THE TRAPPERS I, II, III

214

THESE SCANDALOUS STREETS I, II, III

FEAR MY GANGSTA I, II, III IV, V

THESE STREETS DON'T LOVE NOBODY I, II

BURY ME A G I, II, III, IV, V

A GANGSTA'S EMPIRE I, II, III, IV

THE DOPEMAN'S BODYGAURD I II

THE REALEST KILLAZ I II III

THE LAST OF THE OGS I II III

Tranay Adams

THE STREETS ARE CALLING

Duquie Wilson

MARRIED TO A BOSS I II III

By Destiny Skai & Chris Green

KINGZ OF THE GAME I II III IV V

Playa Ray

SLAUGHTER GANG I II III

RUTHLESS HEART I II III

By Willie Slaughter

FUK SHYT

By Blakk Diamond

DON'T F#CK WITH MY HEART I II

By Linnea

ADDICTED TO THE DRAMA I II III

IN THE ARM OF HIS BOSS II

By Jamila

YAYO I II III IV

A SHOOTER'S AMBITION I II

BRED IN THE GAME

By S. Allen

TRAP GOD I II III

Robert Baptiste

RICH $AVAGE
By Troublesome
FOREVER GANGSTA
GLOCKS ON SATIN SHEETS I II
By Adrian Dulan
TOE TAGZ I II III
LEVELS TO THIS SHYT I II
By Ah'Million
KINGPIN DREAMS I II III
By Paper Boi Rari
CONFESSIONS OF A GANGSTA I II III IV
By Nicholas Lock
I'M NOTHING WITHOUT HIS LOVE
SINS OF A THUG
TO THE THUG I LOVED BEFORE
By Monet Dragun
CAUGHT UP IN THE LIFE I II III
THE STREETS NEVER LET GO
By Robert Baptiste
NEW TO THE GAME I II III
MONEY, MURDER & MEMORIES I II III
By **Malik D. Rice**
LIFE OF A SAVAGE I II III
A GANGSTA'S QUR'AN I II III
MURDA SEASON I II III
GANGLAND CARTEL I II III
CHI'RAQ GANGSTAS I II III
KILLERS ON ELM STREET I II III
JACK BOYZ N DA BRONX I II III
A DOPEBOY'S DREAM

The Streets Never Let Go

By **Romell Tukes**
LOYALTY AIN'T PROMISED I II
By Keith Williams
QUIET MONEY I II III
THUG LIFE I II III
EXTENDED CLIP I II
By **Trai'Quan**
THE STREETS MADE ME I II III
By **Larry D. Wright**
THE ULTIMATE SACRIFICE I, II, III, IV, V, VI
KHADIFI
IF YOU CROSS ME ONCE
ANGEL I II
IN THE BLINK OF AN EYE
By **Anthony Fields**
THE LIFE OF A HOOD STAR
By Ca$h & Rashia Wilson
THE STREETS WILL NEVER CLOSE
By K'ajji
CREAM I II
By Yolanda Moore
NIGHTMARES OF A HUSTLA I II III
By King Dream
CONCRETE KILLA I II
By Kingpen
HARD AND RUTHLESS I II
MOB TOWN 251
THE BILLIONAIRE BENTLEYS
By Von Diesel
GHOST MOB

Stilloan Robinson

MOB TIES I II III

By SayNoMore

BODYMORE MURDERLAND I II III

By Delmont Player

FOR THE LOVE OF A BOSS

By C. D. Blue

MOBBED UP I II III

By King Rio

KILLA KOUNTY

By Khufu

MONEY GAME

By Smoove Dolla

A GANGSTA'S KARMA

By FLAME

BOOKS BY LDP'S CEO, CA$H

TRUST IN NO MAN

TRUST IN NO MAN 2

TRUST IN NO MAN 3

BONDED BY BLOOD

SHORTY GOT A THUG

THUGS CRY

THUGS CRY 2

THUGS CRY 3

TRUST NO BITCH

TRUST NO BITCH 2

TRUST NO BITCH 3

TIL MY CASKET DROPS

RESTRAINING ORDER

RESTRAINING ORDER 2

IN LOVE WITH A CONVICT

LIFE OF A HOOD STAR

Robert Baptiste

9 781955 270533